These delightful romantic classics have been specially reprinted under Fawcett's new Coventry line.

They represent the best of the genre, proven authors who have become immensely popular over the years.

For those who have long loved tales of the Regency period as well as those newly enamored of them, these enduring romances represent a rich reading experience.

Look for new and enthralling titles available each month from Fawcett Coventry.

Also by Claudette Williams:

AFTER THE STORM	23938	$1.75
MYRIAH	23577-7	$1.50
SPRING GAMBIT	23891	$1.75
SUNDAY'S CHILD	23986	$1.75

Buy them at your local bookstore or use this handy coupon for ordering.

COLUMBIA BOOK SERVICE (a CBS Publications Co.)
32275 Mally Road, P.O. Box FB, Madison Heights, MI 48071

Please send me the books I have checked above. Orders for less than 5 books must include 75¢ for the first book and 25¢ for each additional book to cover postage and handling. Orders for 5 books or more postage is FREE. Send check or money order only.

Cost $_____   Name _____

Postage_____   Address _____

Sales tax*_____   City _____

Total $_____   State _____ Zip _____

*The government requires us to collect sales tax in all states except AK, DE, MT, NH and OR.

This offer expires 1/30/81

Jewelene

Claudette Williams

FAWCETT COVENTRY • NEW YORK

*To my cousin Cheryl
with love.*

JEWELENE

Published by Fawcett Coventry Books, a unit of CBS Publications, the Consumer Publishing Division of CBS Inc.

Copyright © 1979 by Claudette Williams

ALL RIGHTS RESERVED

ISBN: 0-449-50060-8

Printed in the United States of America

First Fawcett printing: February 1979

10 9 8 7 6 5 4 3 2

One

"Someone once told me that the road to Hell was paved with good intentions! Fiend seize me if I haven't just cut such a path!" growled the Marquess of Lyndhurst, kicking a well-appointed stool for emphasis.

His cousin, the Honorable Oscar Robendale, gave him a rather blank stare and reached for his glass of sherry. He dared not question the volatile marquess when he was in such a mood.

"She has tricked me again! Bless her, Rob, for the best of good mothers. I'd swear there was none sweeter or finer in all Albion, but . . . but . . ." He seethed for lack of a proper description of his present opinion of his only surviving parent.

"Wants you neatly married . . . wants grandchildren . . . only natural you know," offered his cousin unwisely.

"Married—aye, she wants that!" said his lordship drily. He moved to the great marble fireplace and, placing his elbow on the shelf, touched his thumb and knuckle to his sensuous mouth. He lost himself in thought. His mother had presented him with yet another challenge—one that he had taken up only to find it irritating beyond endurance.

The Honorable Oscar Robendale fell into studied quiet as he stared at the back of the marquess's ginger-colored locks. Surely the marquess was in a greater temper than usual. After all, it wasn't the first time his lordship's mama had sent some fluttering virgin his way. Why so hot about it? He ventured a query regarding this, only to regret his folly almost immediately, for the marquess rounded on him, his gray eyes on fire. "Yes, wonder at it, Robby! Never was a grown man plagued as I—and all in the name of love! Does my upcoming attainment of the magical year of thirty mean I am in danger of senility?" spluttered his lordship, much affected by such a notion.

"No, no, dear boy. Don't think m'aunt had senility in mind . . . really old fellow," hastily offered his cousin, "told you . . . she wants grandchildren . . . you being the heir and all. Well . . . it stands to reason, don't it?"

"Yes, and so she shall get them—when I am ready!" snapped his lordship.

"Thing is . . . you will be thirty inside of three months."

"And what does that signify?"

"Well . . . don't know about these things . . . never fostered a brat and have a year or two before I reach thirty m'self," explained Robby somewhat disjointedly. "But . . . could be . . . just could be that it's harder to . . . father a brat after you've hit thirty." He frowned and, before his lordship could bring down the scalding retort he had in mind, added, "But don't think that's so. Old MacBee, he's at least forty if he is a day and has a regular brood . . . and there's Sir Thomas . . . didn't marry till he was five and thirty, and he has a brat or two . . . quite sure of it, and there . . ."

"Fiend seize it, Rob, do shut up! I have no need for you to enumerate every father who is past thirty. It doesn't matter anyway. I've agreed to her scheme," interrupted the marquess.

Robendale's hazel eyes showed promise of enlarging considerably. "What's that you say? You dog! Going to tie the knot? And all this while never letting on! You . . ."

"Shut up, Robby! Tie the knot indeed. Noddy! How you came to be in the family is beyond me."

"Shouldn't be. Thought you understood. Your mother and mine are first cousins . . . that makes us . . ."

"Never mind!" spluttered his lordship, nearly beside himself. "I'm in for it now, old friend. But I daresay it shan't be more than a few days' inconvenience. And there will be your company to while away the hours . . . God help me."

"Of course, my company. Happy to be of assistance," said Robby without pausing to think. However, as he finished his sentence his eyes took on a wary look, "What do you mean, Keith?"

"Mean . . . what should I mean?"

"Don't know really . . . never do! Should like to—I think—but there, you were ever a mysterious fellow."

"The thing is, Rob, that she has found me yet another virgin; however, this time the girl shan't be coming to London to parade herself before me for approval. *I* am expected to go to *her* . . . and she, little bumpkin, dwells on the Isle of Wight!"

"Upon my soul!" breathed his cousin, evidently thinking this beyond belief, "does she really . . . why?"

From the look his lordship cast his younger cousin, one would hardly suspect that the Honorable Oscar Robendale held a very high place in his esteem. However, it had been Keith's habit to whip the reins over Robby since childhood. They had grown up quite in each other's way, and Keith's nature and age had made him the leader. However, he summoned enough patience to explain further:

"Listen carefully, Rob, and I shall endeavor to make it plain. M'mother commanded my presence at Berkley this morning. As she has been out of town . . . on that blasted isle this last month, I thought it my duty—indeed was inclined—to see the sly little love! So, rather unwisely, I obeyed. Within ten minutes I began to realize she was up to one of her tricks. Knew it the minute she began vaporing over her poor departed Delia Henshaw and the lovely children that lady left behind. The only odd thing about it is that it would appear from all she has told me that these Henshaws seem to be in straitened circumstances. You know mother has never been a mercenary sort. But still, all the chits she has flung in my path previously have come from fairly affluent and notable families. Well, never mind . . . " he sighed. "I don't know what she is about in that direction, but it ended thusly—a promise from me to visit with the Henshaws and look over the chit, who, by the way, is not in her first bloom. The girl is one and twenty! Now I ask you, Rob . . . what is mother about sending me after a chit past her prime and still unattached?"

"Odd that," answered Robby thoughtfully. He sipped a bit more sherry and stared at a brass button on the marquess's blue superfine coat. "But . . . you know, Keith . . . the dowager has never pitted any but the finest looking chits at you before. Really . . . each and every one a diamond. . . ."

"Yes, I know. But one and twenty . . . there must be something wrong with her."

"Aye, she lives on that God-forsaken isle—that's what!"

"And that's where *we* are going," returned the marquess, smiling for the first time.

Robendale rose to his feet and declared firmly, *"Not I!"*

"Do sit down and calm yourself. It was the only way. I told you m'mother offered me a *deal* of sorts. I promised her to have a go . . . to look over the Henshaw wench in return for her promise to let me be!"

"No? Really? Never say she agreed to that," said Robby, momentarily diverted.

"She did," replied the other proudly.

"Well then, plain as pikestaff this chit is more than meets the eye. She might just nabble you, Keith," said Robby with some concern. "Better not go."

"Ha! I haven't been caught yet. Not a one . . . and, I must admit, her selection has been quite . . . exquisite. But nary a one managed to move me. How could they? Robby, have you any idea what it is to know that when a pretty girl looks your way, it is because you have a title and an immense fortune?"

"How would I know? For one thing, don't have a title or any sort of wealth . . . in dun territory more times than I like to think on . . . and besides not in the petticoat line!" he patted his substantial belly. "Plump, you know. Like it, mind, enjoy m'food, always will. But the chits—they take to a plump man only if his plumpness extends to his pockets!"

"Exactly my point," agreed his lordship contemptuously. "Mercenary little things, each and every one of 'em!"

"Aye, but it's different with you, Keith. I'll warrant you the wenches would wink in your direction even if your pockets were to let. I mean . . . you ain't given over to fat. Good Lord! Just look at you!"

It was true, the Marquess of Lyndhurst was a great figure of a man. His ginger-colored hair was sparked with gold. The thick waving locks reached down to his broad shoulders. His gray eyes were bright with sharp wit and set off by dark lashes and straight thick brows. His nose, though prominent, was strongly masculine above a well-shaped, sensuous mouth, and his height and hardness of muscle were such as to make a lady eye him with considerable interest. Too bad that such a specimen should be a cynic! But a cynic he was especially with women!

It had started some nine years before when he was but twenty, in the bloom of youth. He had at that sensitive time in life fancied himself in love with a shopkeeper's daughter.

It had caused his parents much grief and many sleepless nights. His father, a man of means and know-how, discovered that his heir meant to marry a tradesman's spawn. This mésalliance would have destroyed Keith's social standing forever, and his father had no intention of allowing his only son to commit such folly.

The late marquess made inquiries regarding the girl and, much to his pleasure, discovered that she was quite a coquette. She had a lover, and her heart was certainly pledged, but not to Keith. It was inevitable that when Keith's father offered her ten thousand pounds to run off with her lover (an actor of some talent) she seized the opportunity greedily—a foolish thing, to be sure, considering what she was throwing away. However, she had no assurance that she could make young Keith marry her, and she was not sure that his powerful father could not bring about the annulment he threatened if she dared to marry his son. In addition to this, she was truly in love with her actor.

Thus it was that Keith gained some sophistication, for his father did not spare him the details. The late marquess thought it best to let his son know just what sort of woman he had been dealing with. He meant for his son to walk the earth with his eyes wide open, and Keith took it hard —too hard. His eyes did open—perhaps too wide. Odd what distortions bitterness can produce. It was easy after such a blow to find something wrong with each and every woman he came across.

"Humph! You are just a lad. You know nothing of women!" said the marquess.

"I am seven and twenty. Fat I may be, but I've had m'fair share. Said I wasn't in line, and so I ain't. But that don't make me an innocent!" snapped his cousin, much affronted.

"Course it don't, noddy. Only meant . . . you've never had your heart involved."

"Don't signify. Still say . . ."

"I know, that's because you are at heart a romantic!" chuckled the marquess.

"Romantic indeed! Level-headed . . . anyone will tell you I'm level-headed. Just know what I know," returned Robby, taking a seat again.

"And what do you know?"

"That I ain't getting involved. That's what. I ain't going with you to that bedeviled isle, and that's the end of it!"

Two

The Henshaw house was situated at the top of a clear knoll. Only scattered elms and pines broke the starkness of the landscape surrounding its Tudor lines. What had once been a magnificently maintained park was now being allowed to run to weeds, for its present inhabitants had not a penny to their name.

However, young Sir James and his sister, Jewelene Henshaw, were optimists at heart. They never allowed the shabbiness of the home they loved to weigh them down for more than a moment or two, and both worked toward reviving its previous glory.

Sir James, who was eighteen months younger than his twenty-one-year-old sister, had some time back hatched up a scheme. Jewelene had taken to his notion, and they were now seeing the fruition of their plans. Dressed in shabby buckskin jackets and breeches, they sat upon the pen fence and watched as their old groom, Jonas, led a magnificent black Arabian stallion toward them.

"I say, Jewelene, he'll do . . ." exclaimed Sir James, thwacking his knee for emphasis.

Jewelene brushed long honey-gold hair away from her eyes and cooed to the horse. The stallion flicked his ears and nodded his head. This made her brother laugh. "Look at that! He knows us!"

"He should—after all the training we've given him," she replied emphatically.

"Aye, that's the truth," he agreed.

She glanced wistfully above his curly light brown hair.

"If only we can get a win at Derby . . . imagine, Jimmy . . . just imagine how much we could make with Lightning as a breeder!"

"Aye. Trouble is . . . he's ready, but *we* ain't. Face it, girl, we still have to meet the entrance fee."

"We shall. If I have to marry that wretched creature, Omsbury, to get it . . ."

"I'd as lief sell my soul to the devil as let you marry that rum touch! I won't have it," declared her brother.

"But, Jimmy, you should be at Cambridge with your friends . . . not here, worrying about the estate. He is willing to give you a handsome marriage settlement."

"And you loathe the ground he walks upon. What pleasure would there be for me, knowing you made such a match? Plague take him!"

"All right, all right," she said, hastily interrupting him, for he showed signs of going off into an apoplexy over the matter. "I will just have to think of another way."

"That's my job, not yours! We still have two weeks."

" 'Tis not long. But never mind, I daresay we shall come about, we have always."

Sir James looked up at the sky, and the sun's position told him he had already disregarded his aunt's wishes. She had expressly charged him to bring his sister home in time to change before the Marquess of Lyndhurst's arrival. He shot his sister a quizzical look. "Lord, girl, you look a sight! Aunt will go into convulsions if you should walk in on the marquess looking like that."

"Oh, pooh! Besides . . . he will probably be late. All marquesses arrive late. 'Tis the thing," she bantered.

He laughed. "You know, I rather liked the dowager. She was a right 'un. Mama had a friend in her."

"A rare thing, but you are right there. Do you miss them? Mother and father?"

"Yes," he said quietly.

"Oh, Jim, sometimes . . . it just is so unbearable . . ." she said on half a sob.

"Give over, girl. That won't help. It's been two years since the accident took them . . ."

"I suppose for them . . . it was the best thing. They couldn't have endured separation," she sighed. "Well . . . never mind. Come, we had better get back. I promised Elizabeth to help her arrange the flowers, scarce as they are."

A dark coach bearing the crest of Lyndhurst, together with its horses, luggage, and riding mounts, was resting aboard a schooner in the harbor of Portsmouth. The marquess and his companion, the Honorable Oscar Robendale, stood at the bow, leaning on their elbows. Their capes were flapping in the wind as was their hair beneath their top hats.

"Don't know how you convinced me to do this!" grumbled Robendale, though secretly he was now beginning to enjoy the journey. He liked the feel of the salt air stinging his face; and the fact that he had never visited the small diamond-shaped isle off the coast of Hampshire made it all the more exciting.

The marquess laughed. "Give over and admit it, you devil, you are having a splendid time. I let you beat me two rubbers at piquet, didn't I?"

Robby cast him a sharp look but said nothing. He felt the boat move and exclaimed enthusiastically, "We're off!"

"Aye, devil take it, so we are. Lord, I wish I could get out of this."

"Can't," returned Robby practically.

"It's just that I do so dislike being fawned upon and toadied to."

"Don't know they will dangle after you. Might take you in dislike," offered Robby amiably.

The marquess said not a word to this, for his mind had suddenly taken hold of a strong fancy. He had to formulate it, reflect upon it, and so he stared out at the still bay before him. His cousin watched him warily. Robby recognized the look, and it always spelled trouble. Then the marquess's gloved fist smacked his open hand, and he said, "Robby . . . I have it, Robby!"

"You do?" asked Robby cautiously.

"Aye. *You,* Robby, are going to masquerade as *me,*" said the marquess.

Robendale's hazel eyes widened in disbelief. "This thing . . . it has gone to your noodle. Sit down, old friend. Catch your breath . . . here . . . out of the sun. . . ."

"No, no," said the marquess irritably, shrugging off his cousin's solicitous arm. "I am perfectly all right. Just listen to me. You and I shall come to grips on this thing. It will liven up our stay on this God-forsaken isle. Look, Rob, I am willing to put up my hunter on this wager, for I say the Henshaw chit will take to you in spite of your inability to turn a flattering line, and in spite of your . . ."—he patted his cousin's plump paunch—"simply because she will think it is *you* who is the wealthy marquess!"

"You've gone daft, man!" exclaimed Robby hotly. "We don't even look alike."

"It doesn't signify. They have never seen me. It is perfect, Rob. You have tried to make a point, which is that I would still be able to win the chits were I penniless and untitled! Very well, shall we put it to the test? You will be me and I you."

"No! And *I* ain't *always* penniless! Am now because had a bit of ill luck before the quarter, but the next quarter will see me clear again. Have *something* of a living, old boy."

"That doesn't matter," said the marquess impatiently. "What does is that you are only an earl's second son and *not* the heir since your elder brother has children . . . and this living you speak of is not anything to catch a dear maid's eye. Furthermore, I shall be the Honorable Oscar Robendale and just to add a bit of flavor . . . an inveterate gambler to boot!"

"But . . . I should always be letting the thing out of the basket by calling you Keith," pleaded Robby.

"That is easy enough. Call me Keith. I'll call you Roben, they don't know our given names. All they know is m'mother is sending her son the *marquess!*"

"I don't like it, Keith."

"*My hunter*—and you have naught to lose except a drink and an admission that I was right all along," urged the marquess.

The chance of getting a prime blood away from his cousin dangled clearly before Rob's watery gaze. "Your hunter, you say . . . the gray . . . no mistake?"

"Aye, m'hunter. Is it a wager then?"

"Done!" said Robendale, feeling somehow that he had sealed an unhappy fate for himself.

At the Henshaw house, Mrs. Debbs, the late Lady Henshaw's sister, paced about the parlor. Her lavender silks rustled about her short plump figure. She spied her daughter sitting serenely with her embroidery and let out an exasperated sigh. "My word, Elizabeth, I should think you would at least show some interest!"

Her daughter raised soft brown eyes. She was a slender girl, quietly pretty, whose gentleness had won a warm welcome in the Henshaw household. However her more erratic though dynamic mama was wont to see this characteristic as a fault. Mrs. Dora Debbs had come to Henshaw House with her only surviving child two years ago, after the Henshaws' accident. She had always been close to both her sister and brother-in-law, and their death had been a terrible blow. She loved her sister's children and wished to help them in any way she could but, alas, her own fortune was not very much better than theirs.

"Interest in what, mama?" asked Elizabeth quietly.

"Faith, child! I have told you the Marquess of Lyndhurst will be arriving soon and . . . just look at you! Could you not find a brighter gown? I do so dislike this dove color you seem to prefer."

"Mama, my gown is both serviceable and pretty. What is wrong with the shade? It is soft . . . and, besides, it is Jewelene we wish him to notice."

"That is quite true, child, but Jewelene is . . . Jewelene, and it may be that she may not . . . encourage his interest. Or he may not find her to his taste . . ."

"Oh, mama!" scoffed Elizabeth without bitterness. She was a practical-minded girl. "What man would cast his eyes my way once he has seen Jewelene?"

Mrs. Debbs cast an appraising look over her daughter. Elizabeth had long, fawn-colored hair. Certainly its texture and shine were nothing to scorn. Her soft grace became her, and she was still youthful, having not yet attained her twentieth year. However, she was quite right. In comparison to Jewelene, whose honey-gold hair, sea green eyes, and bouncing form stole hearts without effort on her part, Elizabeth was scarcely noticeable. Jewelene had remained unattached but for three reasons: she had refused the local vicar, John Hopps, four times in the past two years; her only other suitor, Lord Omsbury, was not a desirable match; and her lack of dowry precluded much chance of her getting other offers.

It was a sad trial indeed for Mrs. Debbs whose vitality lent itself to schemes for finding husbands for her daughter and niece. At least her Liz had a dowry of sorts left to her by the late Mr. Debbs. Poor Jewelene had only her looks to launch her—and on the little Isle of Wight there were not very many takers.

"Never mind such talk!" reassured her mother. "You are very lovely, Elizabeth, and in your own way . . ." There was no time to say more as the elderly servant, Stanton, appeared to announce the arrival of the marquess.

Mrs. Debbs looked up somewhat startled. Good God! Here already? It wasn't yet even tea time. She had not expected them until then. Where the deuce was Jewelene . . . and may heaven preserve, she wished her niece would go straight to her room and wash.

The "marquess," looking somewhat sheepish, his long fair hair waving to his shoulders, stepped into the room. His cousin, "the Honorable 'Keith' Robendale," nearly a half foot taller and far more attractive, followed.

Mrs. Debbs went forward to greet them. Her daughter halted her sewing and looked up to smile as her mother presented her. The marquess smiled lamely and took up a seat. His cousin put up a gold-rimmed quizzing glass and asked languidly where Miss Henshaw was hiding herself.

"My . . . my . . . niece?" returned Mrs. Debbs, "Why, she is out with her brother. Though I expect she will arrive shortly." She returned her attention to the marquess, and his cousin smiled to himself.

As Mrs. Debbs became involved in the hearty business of putting the shy marquess at his ease and bringing her equally diffident daughter to his attention, the Honorable Keith Robendale was free to cast his eyes about. The gold silk hangings were the first of the room's furnishings to catch his inquiring eye. They were faded and showed signs of wear as did much of the once elegant furniture. There was still much about the estate and the house that spoke of better days. He wondered what had brought about the Henshaws' ill fortune. From what he had seen of the tenant farmers on their journey, he was quite sure the good people who tilled Henshaw land did not suffer. Odd that.

It was something of a puzzle, and it piqued his interest. Really, he told himself, he shouldn't hold it against the gray-haired but lively Mrs. Debbs for hoping to secure good matches for her daughter and her niece. It was after all the way of the *ton*. Marriages of convenience were the norm, yet he loathed the notion.

A door opened behind him, and his ginger head went round at the sound that followed. It was a winged sound, a bright, merry ring of laughter, and his gray eyes looked up to find two very shabbily dressed young adults. A lad, somewhat above average height, on the lean and lanky side with a pleasant oval-shaped face and a mass of wavy brown hair, stepped in.

At his side was a remarkable, though somewhat odd, female. Her exceptionally long hair flowed in vibrant waves to her small waist. It was the color of wild dark honey, richly textured, and wondrously thick. Her cherry lips were curved in a warm smile, her green eyes sparkled as though amused with the scene before her. And her figure—he could not help noting that her form even in the buckskin jacket and breeches looked far more seductive than most women did in full ball dress. To top all this, she seemed not at all distressed to be seen thus.

At the heels of these two merry individuals was a huge black-and-white harlequin Great Dane. Its tongue lolled as it pranced, and it made its way first to the plump young man, eying him rather dubiously. The dog's nose sniffed Roben's hessians.

"Oh . . . oh . . . nice dog . . ." said Robby, his brows going up with some concern.

The animal took this as an invitation to further their acquaintance. He rather liked this fair, pleasant-faced newcomer and proceeded to rise and place his two front paws on Robby's rounded shoulders, matching him in height. This produced a startled exclamation not only from Robby, but from the assembled company. The dog immediately thought it wise to display to all concerned that he offered only friendship; this he did by painting Robby's face with his wide pink tongue.

"No!" cried Jewelene, laughter nearly choking her. "Down, you horrid Caesar! Down! Do you hear?"

"Indeed!" agreed Sir James jumping over a stool in his haste to reach the dog before Caesar's victim took it into his head to seek retribution. "Down, you brute!"

Poor Caesar, finding himself the object of attack, thought it best to make good his escape. The fact that a full-grown man stood directly in his path seemed no deterrent at all. The enormous dog took a leap, sending the plump marquess backwards onto the sofa with an astonished cry.

By this time Sir James had come round to meet his dog face to face. Master and dog eyed one another a moment before Caesar gave way and surrendered. He whined fretfully, aware that somehow he had offended, and dropped in total capitulation to his belly, wherefrom he gave over a series of cries. He sounded very much like a puppy though he had three years to his credit.

"Bad dog!" admonished Sir James roughly.

Caesar placed his head between his front paws and continued to advise his master how sorry he was (noting at the same moment that he had managed to capture the attention of the entire company) and wagged his tail. Sir James still cast him darkling looks of disapproval, so the poor dog took to crawling toward his master on his belly.

"Oh, poor brute . . . there now. He didn't mean it . . . did you, dog?" said Robby sympathetically, feeling somehow guilty.

For answer Caesar yelped, and everyone broke into laughter. Sir James grinned, ordered his pet to remain seated in the corner of the room, and returned his attention to his guests. Coming forward to the two standing gentlemen, he extended his hand, "Hello . . . so sorry, we didn't have a chance to introduce ourselves and give you a proper welcome. I am Sir James Henshaw, and this is m'sister, Jewelene. Daresay you've already met m'aunt Dora . . . and her daughter, Elizabeth Debbs?"

Robby gulped and eyed his cousin miserably, for what had been a simple (though delicate) lark of sorts now seemed somehow wretchedly wicked. These were nice people though, to be sure, the Henshaw chit certainly had a hoydenish manner of dressing. Nonetheless . . . that was no excuse for deceiving them. He mumbled something about being happy to meet them and allowed Keith to take over the conversation.

Keith had witnessed the entire episode as though one watching a comic play. He took no part, yet managed to enjoy himself thoroughly. This visit with the Henshaws might turn out to be a great deal less insipid than he had earlier imagined, and the Henshaw chit intrigued him. She seemed not at all interested in the fact that she was dressed most improperly for anywhere—let alone her own drawing room. Yet she had an air of self-assurance and confidence about her.

He bowed to her and, as his cousin seemed unable to present him, he did the job himself. "I am the marquess's cousin, Keith Robendale, and I am delighted at this opportunity to spend time with such a charming host . . ." —he cast his eyes over Jewelene— "and hostess." He meant to flirt, believing she would turn a cold shoulder, and felt more than half surprised when she smiled warmly at him.

"Do resume your seats, gentlemen," said Jewelene sweetly, "I shall ring for tea." She glanced at her white-faced aunt who had still to regain her composure and speech, and once again the real marquess of Lyndhurst was treated to a pair of twinkling green eyes.

Three

Aunt Dora's hazel eyes nearly popped as she gasped, "Jewelene..." then remembering their guests, she lowered her voice, "dearest, surely you don't mean ... to stay to tea as well ... you must go up and change ... *at once!*"

Jewelene lowered her voice. "No, Aunt Dora, I shall be going out again in a short while, so it would be silly to change just for tea."

Aunt Dora smiled apologetically at their guests before continuing. "Well ... I daresay ... you didn't realize the marquess and his cousin had arrived. ..."

"Oh, but they told us in the stables that they had arrived," interjected Sir James, beaming. "Jewelene thought it best that we march right in and give you our welcome."

Aunt Dora looked murderously his way, and Sir James's jaw dropped for he was now sure of a growing suspicion—their loving aunt was somehow most put out with them. He stared askance at her while Jewelene directed her speech to Roben sitting opposite her. "My brother is quite right you know. We couldn't wait to come and wish Lady Lyndhurst's son welcome. I must tell you that your mama quite captivated our hearts, we hated to see her go; but your being here now will bring her back to us. She is quite a lively lady and it was great fun hearing the many tales she had of our mother. It seems the two of them were rather mischievous in their youth."

Robby blushed profusely and knew not what to say, so acute was his embarassment. He looked toward his cousin who came quickly to the rescue. "Indeed . . . the dowager has still that bewitching quality," said Keith.

Jewelene gave Roben a thoughtful look, for she was surprised by the sudden color that flooded his white cheeks. Odd, she thought, whatever did I say to make him blush? She then looked toward Keith and noticed for the first time that here was quite an attractive male figure.

The tea tray was brought in at this moment, giving them the necessary interruption, and all the company (especially Sir James who attacked the offering with gusto) relaxed with their refreshments in hand.

A sigh went round before Aunt Dora broke the silence with a low question, "Jewelene dear . . . you mentioned going out again? Surely that horse has had enough training for one day?"

"Oh, indeed, we shan't be schooling Lightning anymore . . . but we have something of an errand . . . we shan't be long . . ." said Jewelene, hoping her aunt would ask no more questions in front of their guests.

"Errand? What sort? Oh, Jewelene, you don't mean to visit that Clay family again?" she asked with some annoyance.

Jewelene blushed and said quietly, "Aunt Dora, Mrs. Clay is a friend—it is only right . . . at any rate, do not let us quibble now."

Her aunt shot her a look of disapproval, but she thought it best to accede to her niece's request. However, the real marquess of Lyndhurst gazed at Jewelene for a long moment. Really, he had to own that his mother had this time set him against an incomparable. She was certainly different!

"May I ask what sort of blood you are schooling?" asked Keith, his eyes on Jewelene's face.

"Lightning is a pure Arabian. My father made the purchase . . . just before his death . . ." she said turning away slightly. She recovered herself. "He is fast. Really fast. We hope to have him ready for the Derby this month."

"Arabian, eh? They make good show horses . . . strong in the work, but I'd not pit an Arabian against a thoroughbred . . ." answered Roben.

"That is because you have not seen Lightning at his paces!" retorted Jewelene. She then glanced at the clock on the mantel shelf and put up her hands. "My word! I am sorry . . . but I must ask you to excuse us, my lord . . . Mr. Robendale . . ." she said getting to her feet.

The gentlemen all rose hastily, Roben nearly spilling his tea in the process.

"Come on, Jimmy . . . we've got to run if we are to be back by dinner!"

"Right," agreed her brother. Caesar rose to a sitting position and wagged his tail hopefully but his master frowned at him. "No, brute. You are not coming! Stay and keep our guests company."

Jewelene pitied him and bent to pat his head on her way out, giving Keith an admirable vision of her lovely proportions. Then as suddenly as they had appeared, the Henshaws were gone.

Keith and Roben exchanged glances as did Aunt Dora and her quiet daughter. Caesar crossed the room and went directly to Roben where he sighed and placed his huge head upon Roben's hessian. He had somehow and for a reason known only to himself adopted the gentle Roben.

"Well," started Aunt Dora, attempting a recovery, "I . . . I daresay you gentlemen would like to retire to your rooms and relax a bit before dinner. I shall ring for Stanton to show you the way."

Jewelene and her brother rode through the fields towards Yarmouth village. "You know, Jimmy . . . I *am* a little concerned about you and Lyla . . ."

"Are you? Why?" said Jimmy.

"Well, the thing is, when we are rich again, I want you to continue your studies at Cambridge . . ."

"And what has Lyla to do with that?"

"Oh, now, Jimmy, don't play the dunce with me! It won't fadge," said Jewelene impatiently.

He laughed. "Lyla has no place in m'future, Jewel. Lord, I've known the chit half m'life. What? Think I mean to seduce her and then get snabbled? Not me! Don't think of her as a woman."

Jewelene looked somewhat startled, for Lyla Clay was a rather attractive little brunette. "But Jimmy . . ."

"Lord, Jewel . . . she ain't in m'style. Not at all! I like 'em tall, thin, and sweet, and Lyla . . . well . . . she is round, small, and sly! Fun, mind you . . . but not in m'style."

"Hmmm," said Jewelene thoughtfully.

"And what about you and Ben?" teased her brother.

"What is that supposed to mean?" she answered haughtily.

"Now don't try to gammon me that we are going to the Clays to check in on poor Mrs. Clay. You might be able to bamboozle m'aunt with such fustian, *but not me!*"

"Well, 'tis true. I've been wanting to see Ben . . . but not . . . not because of what you think, silly boy! Why, Ben is nearly five and thirty . . . and besides . . . I've never thought of him in such a way, and I am certain he has never thought of . . . Oh! Horrid Jimmy! You are just trying to get me miffed!" She ended for she had caught the light in his eye.

They had already reached the edge of the village, and the sea stretched out a wondrous swirl of greens and blues at their side. Jewelene took a moment to gaze out onto the water and sigh, "Oh, Jim, I do love our sleepy little isle . . . but . . ."

"But you wish you could go to London for a bit of a lark," he ended with a frown. "And I wish it for you, Jewel. But come on . . . we don't want to get too far behind and then be late for dinner. Aunt will have at me—and with cause!"

"Oh, pooh! Imagine . . . I mean, the dowager is sweet to want—really want her son to become interested in me. For with his title and wealth . . . he could have anyone, I daresay."

"Do you think so? He didn't even seem to know how to turn a compliment. Wouldn't think he would get very far with the ladies. Doesn't have the address or style," said her brother thoughtfully.

"Hmm . . . but he is rather sweet, though. I like him," said Jewelene. "But what do you make of his cousin?"

"Eh? That swarthy chap? Now he seems a ladies' man! Fact is, thought him a bit of a rakehell . . . but can't be certain."

"No, we can't pass judgment so quickly, but I do agree with you, Jimmy. He does seem far more sophisticated than his marquess cousin. Why ever did *he* come, I wonder?" she mused.

"Don't know," said her brother, casting his eyes about. They had already arrived at the village square. The battlements of Yarmouth Castle rose above their heads. Tulips adorned the flower beds in the square. People, country types with warm smiles, crowded the streets and presented a very dear, very lovely vision before Jewelene's eyes. Brother and sister traversed the cobbled street to a large, three-story house set back from the main throughfare. Its stone walls were yellowed, its oak lines freshly painted dark brown, and iron railings enclosed its gardens.

A link boy came forward, and they gave their horses into his keeping before crossing the narrow side street and making for this particular house. Sir James rapped vigorously with the door knocker, producing a manservant of some considerable height and girth whose depressing countenance seemed severe in the extreme. A span of many years' faithful service to the Clay family had made him somewhat wary of strangers since the Clays had had their share of ill luck in the past. He trusted few. However, his lips seemed to part somewhat as he observed the Henshaws on the Clays' front steps, and those that knew him well would have realized that this was a sign of sincere pleasure.

"Good day to you, Wailey!" beamed Sir James, stepping aside to allow his sister admittance before him.

"Good day, Sir James . . . Miss Jewelene," said Wailey, moving out of their path.

"Is Mrs. Clay about?" asked Jewelene.

"No, she is out for the day. Gone to the mainland to visit with her sister."

"And Lyla?" asked Sir James.

"Gone, too."

"Oh, bother!" said Jewelene, "I suppose Mr. Clay took them?"

"No, miss, Mr. Clay is across the street at the Silver Heart."

"Oh, very well. I suppose I shall have to go there to speak with him," sighed Jewel.

"No, oh, no," her brother was moved to utter. "Can't do that! It is all very well for you to go about in breeches, dear girl! Got the poor folk of Wight so befuddled that they think it charming. But even *you* can't go into a gaming hell without losing your all!"

"That is silly, Jimmy. It is Ben's place after all. . . ."

"Don't matter. Can't go in there, and that is that! Come with me. We'll go spend some time with Arthur . . . you'll like that," offered her brother.

She hesitated. "No . . . you go on. I don't want to ruin your enjoyment, and I am sure you and Art will want to discuss that boxing match coming up next week. I shall send round to Ben and ask him to attend me here."

Her brother sighed. He wasn't at all sure it was the correct thing to leave her alone with Ben. But then, Ben was practically an uncle. He had in fact been their father's closest friend. No harm then. Ben wouldn't take advantage of the situation, and he did want to run over to Arthur's. "Oh, all right then. Can you do that, Wailey?" He turned to the huge butler.

"Indeed, sir. Right away," said Wailey, disappearing down the hall.

Jewelene called after him that she would wait in the parlor and then turned to kiss her brother good-by. "Come back for me in an hour's time?"

"Done, m'girl," he said and was gone.

She moved down the dark hall to a set of double oak doors. These opened into a small, cozy room decorated in quiet but rich taste. The Clays had fallen on bad times after the death of Ben's father. The estate had gone to Ben when he was in the army, fighting Boney in Spain. Then in 1809 Ben was wounded severely—a wound that cost him his left arm. When he returned he was despondent and bitter, and it was Jewelene's father who had taken him in hand. Together they worked out a scheme. Jewelene's dad had loaned him a sum to start the Silver Heart—not exactly a genteel trade, but Ben Clay could do nothing else to keep house and home together. Gambling. It was in Ben's blood as it had been in Jewelene's father's blood—as it was in Jewelene's.

She thought about this now with a weary sigh. Gambling—it was her father's last gambling venture that had so depleted their comfortable living. It was not only the cards that so intrigued him for he had been quite successful with the cards—a skill he had passed on, not to his heir, James, but to his daughter, Jewelene. What had been his downfall was his addiction to schemes. The new industrial deals were all too tantalizing. He had often gone from one to the next, but then he had always been there to pick them up again. And then that dreadful accident had put a stop to all that.

The door opened, and Jewelene looked up into the oval face of an attractive man. Gentle brown eyes were set in a pleasant countenance. Silky brown waves were cut in such a way as to make one think the wind had some hand in its style. His shirt points were correctly starched, his neckcloth fashionably tied, his velvet coat well fitted—and Jewelene never noticed anymore that one empty sleeve was folded and pinned at the elbow. His smile was warm and welcoming.

"Jewelene!" he said, tossing his cape and top hat aside to come forward and take her hand.

She allowed him to take off her worn kid gloves and kiss her finger tips, smiling coquettishly up at him.

"Oh sir, you do take the breath away, you handsome devil!" It was a game they played—harmless and safe, and one they both enjoyed. "Why, I can hardly believe 'twas only yesterday we met!" she was teasing, moving to kiss his cheek.

"Now, puss, none of that! What brings you here?" he demanded, turning to his stainwood wall table and a decanter of sherry.

"Ben, I have the solution!" she said, smiling at his back.

He turned and gazed at her a moment before taking a sip of the sherry he held to his lips.

"Do you now? Well then, child, give over."

She got to her feet. "It came to me yesterday when I was in the attic going through mother's clothes. You know, we have the dowager's son staying with us . . . and I thought I'd find a few pretty things . . . but never mind that. I found a lovely black wig, a mask, and a most unusual red ball dress. I remembered that mama had worn the outfit to a masquerade ball . . . oh, many years ago when I was quite young. She went as a Frenchwoman . . . and it came to me . . . so shall I!"

"Ah, of course. And in your own good time you will tell me where it is you will be going as a Frenchwoman?" he said, his brown eyes alive.

"Lyla said you were most distressed over one of your best dealers . . . who left you . . . to get married. She was a most attractive woman and did quite well for the Silver Heart . . ." Jewelene began slowly.

Ben was no fool. He understood at once. "Aha! You realize, of course, that you have gone completely daft!"

"But why? I shall wear the wig and the mask and, oh, Ben, you and papa both said there isn't another female alive who can deal faro as I can!"

"Yes, exactly so! And what sort of friend to your father's memory am I that I should allow you to risk your reputation. Good Lord, Jewelene, take the money. . . ."

"I cannot. We already owe you five hundred pounds. We simply cannot take more. I wish to do this so that I can earn enough to repay you and have enough left over for the entrance fee at Derby. If you will not help me . . . I shall have to turn to Omsbury!"

"Over m'dead body!" said Ben, growing red-faced. "I'd no more let you go to that devil than I would m'own sister, and well you know it! Holding me up, are you, girl? It won't do . . . ain't the gentlemanly thing."

"But I am not a gentleman. I am a lady . . . fighting in the only way left open to me. Oh, Ben, where is the harm?"

"How could you pull it off, Jewel? The men that come to the Silver Heart are locals for the most part. They might recognize you . . . your voice . . ."

"No. They would not. I shall be in disguise . . . and my knowledge of French is quite extensive. I shall put on an excellent accent. See if I don't. I could leave my things here and change before coming to the Silver Heart."

"I don't like it . . ." said Ben.

"But you won't forbid it?"

He sighed. ". . . and Jimmy . . . what does he say?"

"Oh, good Lord! You must not tell him. He wouldn't allow it, and he would be driven to something foolish. He has some noddy notion that as head of the family he should be the one to get the money."

"I see." He sighed again. "I don't like it though, Jewelene. You have forced my hand. But mind now, I reserve the right to end the game whenever I think it getting too close . . ."

"Yes, yes, I agree," she said, giving him a fierce hug. " 'Tis done then?"

" 'Tis done . . . God preserve us this day's work!" he added, looking heavenward.

Four

Keith, Marquess of Lyndhurst, stood apart from the assembled group in the parlor of Henshaw House and studied the fruition of his dealings. Things had not been proceeding according to plan. For one thing Robby was finding it very difficult to play his part. He complained incessantly that he felt a wicked devil for the deception. For another, Jewelene Henshaw was like no other female of his knowledge—a knowledge he considered quite extensive.

These troublesome thoughts had come to mind over dinner, an event that had been—quite surprisingly—fun. There was no other description for it. The food had been simple fare but exceptionally well prepared. The conversation had been varied, informal, and most enjoyable—this due largely to the liveliness of both Jewelene and her brother. Elizabeth Debbs, too, had in her own gentle manner a way of injecting herself in the conversation that Keith found . . . interesting.

His first shock wave had accompanied Jewelene's late entrance on her brother's arm. She was wearing a velvet gown of the same sea green as her eyes. Her honey-colored hair was caught at the top of her head by a green ribbon and fell in ringlets all about her head. Her movements were graceful, and it was a difficult thing indeed to associate her with the roughly clothed hoyden of that afternoon.

He saw before him the wild beauty transformed into a regal goddess and gave silent thanks that he had traded identities with his cousin, Roben. For surely he would be hard put to deny her should she wage a full-scale war for his heart. He then attempted to step back and watch the proceedings as Jewelene began to dazzle poor Roben. This she did with an adroitness he applauded, yet with such little effort that one would hardly suspect her intentions. And still she played the lady—for next she brought Elizabeth to the attention of Roben. Ha! thought Keith. Why not? She had naught to fear there. Elizabeth was fair enough, but what was her gentle loveliness next to Jewelene's entrancing beauty?

Keith's next surprise came at the dinner table. Aunt Dora was seated at one end, Sir James at the other; however, Jewelene had elected to seat Roben beside her cousin, while she took up position beside himself. His brow went up. But then, Sir James and Jewelene's openness of manners set everyone at ease. They had no qualms at directing conversation across the table and did so with happy abandon. Purposely (it seemed to Keith), Jewelene set Elizabeth, her aunt, Roben, and her brother onto a controversial topic—regarding Wilberforce's last essays—and then turned quietly to him.

It was, of course, true. She had set about to engage Keith in solitary conversation. She sensed his withdrawn attitude and meant to ferret him out. "And so . . . Mr. Robendale . . ." said Jewelene giving him a bewitching smile, "we have all said more than is wise about ourselves and yet, you have elected to remain aloof. I have no further on you than I did this afternoon!"

"Ah, but there is really very little about me worth the knowing," he said evasively.

She laughed. "Not true, sir! I see from your excellently cut and well-fitting clothes that you are not only a man of fashion . . . but a corinthian as well. From your knowledge of horseflesh, I would also say you are an accomplished whip . . . and from your eyes . . . oh, now . . . what secrets they hold . . ." She was teasing, drawing him out, meaning only to banter with him. But it took him quite aback.

He stared hard at her a moment before regaining his composure. "Secrets? What possible secrets could I have?"

"May I?" she said, taking up his hand. It was an idle gesture, one she would have done with her brother, with Ben, with any number of local men she knew, yet suddenly at the touch of his strong hand she felt a blush steal into her cheek. However, she would not retract—'twould look idiotic. So she maintained her hold. "Palm reading, sir . . . it tells all."

"Very well, then. Have at me!" he smiled, enjoying this.

"Aha! Your lifeline spells longevity . . . and more. You see these little strokes that cross?" she asked, pointing and making it up as she went along. "These speak of . . . chances. Do you take chances . . . are there mysteries about you, Mr. Robendale, that we know nothing of?"

His brow went up and he marveled at her for a moment. But this was, of course, his opportunity. He had been waiting for an occasion to confess himself an incorrigible gambler, a penniless spendthrift. It was essential to the wager with his cousin. Very well, little flirt, he thought, let us see if you are still interested after you hear this.

"How astute of you, my pretty, though it is no mystery. I am a gamester."

"Really!" said she, surprised in turn. She was just about to mention her own fallibility in this regard but then thought better of it. She looked him straight in the eyes—

and really one must applaud his lordship's ability to carry off the lie for he did so without flinching. "Whatever will you do away from your hells in London?"

"Oh, I imagine I shall find a gaming house somewhere on this heathenish isle . . ." he answered with a mock show of ennui.

"Lord, yes," said Sir James, coming in on the conversation suddenly. "You must visit the Silver Heart in Yarmouth. They even have a faro table there . . . and you will be pleasantly surprised to find the stakes can match any of the hells in London," he concluded proudly.

"I doubt that," responded Keith. "But I most certainly will look in on them." He then glanced at Jewelene's face and was surprised to note a look of slight consternation in her green eyes.

And now, standing apart from them all, watching her as she organized their evening's entertainment, he wondered what that look could signify. The girl had secrets of her own, and he wondered once again how she had reached the age of one-and-twenty and had not yet caught a husband. Odd that.

"All right then, it is settled . . . we'll play Derby run!" cried Sir James with much excitement. "Come on, Lizzie girl, 'tis all the crack!"

"But I am unsure . . ." Liz began.

"Don't worry, dear . . . I'll show you the way of it. We can play partners if you like and make Aunt Dora deal," offered Jewelene.

"Oh, yes, I should like that—just until I acquire the knack of it, Jewel," answered Liz.

"By Jove, yes!" agreed Roben pleasantly. " 'Tis devilishly good fun, though I haven't played it since Christmas with the boys . . ." He suddenly went silent.

"Boys?" queried Jewelene at once. "I understood you were an only child."

"Well, yes, but m'cousin there . . . he has an older brother . . . and we and their children . . ." floundered Roben, flushing dark red.

Keith stepped in hastily to rescue the situation. "My brother has numerous offspring. We were at their estate in Hampshire for the holidays. We played Derby run at that time."

"Oh . . . of course," said Jewelene, wondering why Robby was looking so purplish.

Derby run was a horse race run with cards. It was fast-paced, undeniably childish, and total fun. Four aces signified horses, which the assembled group took some fuss and time naming. The deck was then shuffled and cut, and six cards were dealt face up in a column on one side of the four horses.

The object was to shuffle the remaining cards, turning them up one by one, allowing the ace (horse) of the same suit to advance one step each time its suit showed. The first ace (horse) to make the six steps was, of course, the winner.

Bets were placed, and hooting, rooting, and howling had begun when Stanton entered and announced Lord Reginald Omsbury. All heads turned as a man of average height and build entered. He was well dressed in a gray superfine. His black hair touched with gray was cut à la Brutus, and his dark eyes were set deep in a not unattractive face. He went forward first to Mrs. Debbs and took her hand, murmuring something low. Then adroitly managing to ignore the remaining people with the exception of one, he made his way to Miss Henshaw, drawing her up from the floor and placing a far too warm kiss upon her white hand.

"Jewelene, as always—you are enchanting!"

"And, my lord, as always . . . though gallant, you are far too bold," she said sweetly. Without waiting for his reply she turned towards the others. "My lord, allow me to make you known to our guests. You may recall meeting the dowager Lady Lyndhurst. Well, I am pleased to make her son the marquess . . . " she said indicating Roben, "known to you . . . as well as his cousin, Keith Robendale. His lordship Reginald Omsbury . . ."

Omsbury's estates were situated on the Isle of Wight. However, he was well affluenced and until this past year had spent most of his time in London where he maintained a town house. It was, of course, his desire to make Jewelene his wife that had kept him close to the isle. Though he had never met the Marquess of Lyndhurst, he was well acquainted with that notable's reputation. The stout young man blushing before him fit none of the stories he had heard. This was no rakehell . . . this was no corinthian. Then he saw Keith Robendale, the marquess's cousin, and he glanced again at the ginger head of hair, attempting to recall something . . . but it quite slipped his mind. At any rate, what did it matter to him?

He turned his attention once again to Jewelene and ignored her frowning brother. "Jewelene . . . grant me a moment . . . I would speak with you."

"She don't want to grant you a moment," growled Sir James.

Keith's brows went up. Interesting, this. What was it all about? To keep peace and avoid a scene, Jewelene cast her brother a warning glance. She had no wish to be private with Lord Omsbury who had a knack of frightening her, but she would not allow her brother to dictate to her. "Of course, sir," she said graciously, then turning to the assembled company, "If you will excuse me." She led his lordship out of the room, across the hall, and into the library. She turned, hands on hips, eyes glaring, "Now, my lord, will you tell me why you chose to single me out so pointedly?"

"It has come to my attention that you have gone into debt in order to buy the needed machinery for the mill . . ." he started.

"What has that . . ." demanded Jewelene indignantly.

"Tsk . . . tsk . . . now hear me out before you dress me down, love," he said quietly, being well acquainted with her volatile temper. "I dislike your being in debt to another man. I wish to redeem your notes."

"I don't know how you came to have such information, but the man I am indebted to was a friend of my father's . . . is a friend to me . . ."

"And is heavily in debt himself!" snapped Omsbury. "I told you, Jewelene. I am tired of being patient!" His hand reached out and took hold of her arm, pinching through the velvet. "It has taken me a while, but I have managed to obtain the notes your friend Benjamin Clay was forced to sign this past year in order to bring you and himself about! I hold them over his head as well as yours!"

She yanked free of his grasp. "You fiend! Think you can frighten me with such nonsensical threats? Five hundred is naught to Ben. Why, his place is worth ten times . . ."

"He had some heavy losses . . . to me . . . he is in debt not for five hundred but for five thousand. . . ."

* * *

Keith looked from Aunt Dora to Sir James's youthful and somewhat troubled countenance. There was a tension he could almost feel with a probe. Whatever did this Omsbury hold over them? This was a mystery he couldn't allow to slip by without trying to uncover its roots. He stretched leisurely and broke the stillness of the room.

"Indeed, yes," said Elizabeth with some heat. "He is a horrid man, and I have a good mind to . . ."

"Hush, dear," said her mother, patting her hand. "Jewelene knows best in this matter."

"Yes, but, mama . . ." objected her daughter.

It surprised Keith. He didn't think Elizabeth had it in her to feel so strongly. But it was Sir James who got up from the floor and brushed himself off. "Think I'll just go in . . ."

His aunt pulled at his arm. "She will not like it, James."

"But Aunt . . ."

"I am certain Miss Henshaw would not allow us to yawn from boredom our first night here," said Keith easily. "Don't fret, Sir James. She won't mind *my* fetching her, I think," at which he strolled leisurely across the room.

"Mind me, Jewelene . . . you've teased me long enough! One way or another, I will have you! In the end you will do better for you and yours to give over willingly!" threatened his lordship, his hands going round her trim waist.

Keith heard this last just as his hand went round the gold knob of the library door. Hmm . . . such intrigues in the country? Who would have thought it possible? He stopped, inclined to listen and so satisfy his curiosity.

"Let me go, Omsbury . . . you are a cad! Fiend seize your soul! Let me go . . . do you hear? Shall I call my brother?"

Omsbury laughed—and it was not a nice sound. "You are no fool, Jewelene. Your brother would be honor bound to call me out. I do not think you wish to see him across the dueling field from me!" He was drawing her forcefully against him, his full lips about to close on her mouth.

She struggled in his arms, fighting against his brutish embrace, when all at once he released her.

Keith's eagerness to satisfy his curiosity stopped the moment he realized the man inside was taking unfair advantage of the chit. He opened the door and stepped within, his gray eyes hard as bolts, his jawline set, his dark brows up. "My lord, Sir James wishes his sister to return to the parlor and her aunt immediately. I am certain you have no objection?"

Omsbury was used to getting his own way. He disliked being thwarted and cast Keith a contemptuous look. "You are wrong. I have much objection to Miss Henshaw's leaving my company. But if the lady wishes . . . ?" he challenged Jewelene, his eyes warning her that she had better remain.

But she would not be forced to anything, especially by such a knave. She put up her chin bravely. "The lady wishes!" she hissed and swept past Keith in her hurry to escape.

Keith watched her a moment, wondering why she had accepted a private interview with Omsbury in the first place, before turning to cast disdainful eyes upon his lordship. "I believe, my lord, your business is . . . er . . . quite ended here. I bid you a pleasant evening. Shall I see you to the door?"

"I know the way!" growled Omsbury, but as he reached the library door, he turned to Keith. "Take heed, Mr. Robendale. She is not for your cousin—and she is certainly not for you! There is but one man that Jewelene Henshaw will marry!"

"And he is?" goaded Keith.

"Myself!" snapped Omsbury.

"That is, of course, for the lady to say!" answered Keith. "Good night, my lord." As he watched Omsbury depart, he knew that he had made a dangerous enemy for himself. Well, well, thought he, this stay in the country was proving to be amusing after all.

Five

Keith strode across the dimly lit hall and knocked gently on his cousin's door. There was no response, but that was not unusual considering the fact that it was scarcely seven A.M. He tried the door and was thankful to find it unlocked. Moving in slowly, he found his way to the drapes and drew them wide, allowing the morning's gray light to flood the room. However Robby neither stirred nor showed any sign of awareness.

Keith smiled to himself and crossed to the bed where he proceeded to poke his unsuspecting cousin. "Rob . . . Rob . . ." he whispered.

Robby groaned and opened his eyes. Keith's ginger head came into focus. "Wh . . . at . . . ?"

"Wake up, I want to talk to you," said Keith.

"What . . . what time is it?" asked Robby groggily.

"Five minutes to seven," came the glib answer.

"What?" shrieked Robby, "Never say so! Plague take you, villain. What do you mean waking me at this inhuman hour? Off—off, I say!"

"Robby, do stop blustering and sit up. I want to talk to you. Something has been bothering me all night. Things are not all they seem to be here, you know."

Robby groaned and pushed himself up to a sitting position. He looked so ridiculous with his sleeping cap askew that he made Keith chuckle, which in turn made Rob growl, "You are a dog! An inconsiderate fellow with no scruples. I'll say there's something devilish afoot, and it is all *your* doing. You being me and me being you! Paltry, I say. Ramshackle thing to do. Why, when she asked me about m'mother . . . I mean, your mother . . . I nearly fainted. I tell you . . ."

"Shut up, Rob!" said Keith amiably. He whisked off his cousin's nightcap and sat down upon the bed. "Want to discuss something serious with you."

Robby opened his watery eyes wider and noted for the first time that the marquess was completely dressed. He appraised him not without admiration for the marquess's cravat was expertly tied, his kid waistcoat exactly matched his buckskin riding coat and breeches, and the shine of his hessians was most enviable. "What's this? You dressed, old boy? Are we leaving? Oh, do say we are leaving."

"Leaving? No, I rather think we'll be staying a mite longer now. The Henshaws are a most intriguing pair."

"But there was that Omsbury chap. Dangerous fellow. He is known in every dive and gaming hell in London! We've been introduced to him. Why, this whole thing is getting sticky."

"Don't be a fool, Robby. 'Tis naught but a lark . . . for a wager, and so we shall say, should we have to. At the moment we need not though."

"But don't like bamboozling Mrs. Debbs for one thing. 'Tis . . . 'tis . . ."

" 'Tis much less than you are making it seem!" snapped the marquess impatiently. "Very well, then. If you want out, it is a simple matter. Admit freely that the Henshaw chit has flung her cap your way and not mine!"

"Now . . . what maggot . . . how in all honesty can I do that, Keith? There hasn't been time and, if you ask me, *you* caught her eye, not me!"

"That may be, but it was you she fluttered over. It was you she pranced round. It was . . ."

"You are out there, Keith! The spritely thing prances about simply in the course of things. Doesn't seem to know how to move without dancing. Lovely habit, really, makes one feel . . . festive . . ." Robby mused.

Keith shot him a sharp look. "Careful . . . don't you come under the chit's spell."

"Pshaw! The thing is I can't admit that she is dropping the kerchief m'way . . . and won't admit that she is mercenary!" he said stubbornly.

"Then we'll just have to go through with our wager—which is precisely what I wish, because there are a few things that have me . . . curious."

"Such as?"

"Such as, if she ain't mercenary . . . out for a title, then why don't she send that Omsbury to perdition? I mean, Rob, he insulted her, and though she didn't like it, she did not throw him out. I had to manage the thing!"

"Odd that. When she returned to the parlor after her interview with Omsbury, I thought that brother of hers would burst, he was so done up. He did in fact make for the door, but she put a stop to it," said Robby thoughtfully.

"Yes. I must say her cousin, Elizabeth, showed more spirit than Miss Henshaw in that regard," mused the marquess. "Miss Debbs . . . quite at variance with her cousin, isn't she? Lovely, too. I wonder if mother brought me here to have a look at her? Throwing me off by not mentioning her . . . telling me 'twas the Henshaw chit . . . when in reality 'tis Elizabeth?"

"You think so?" asked Robby, surprised. "I don't. Doesn't make sense. Cunning, though, if it were her purpose; though in truth I don't think Elizabeth Debbs holds a candle to Jewelene Henshaw!"

"Really? I would have thought Elizabeth just in your style," remarked the marquess.

"Just goes to show you, old boy . . . don't know everything, do you? Like 'em lively, full of fun. It's the lively ones that make you happy, you know. They don't sit about and fret . . . forever asking you to do the heart and flowers for 'em, you know. May not be as knowing as you in all matters . . . but that much I learned!" Robby rejoined somewhat pugnaciously.

The marquess grinned broadly and, stretching, got to his feet; however, a movement outside brought him to the window. He gazed down onto the west lawns and watched as Jewelene, a large leather satchel in her hand, sped across the yard.

Without a word he turned on his heel and made for the door. Robby watched him in some disbelief. "I say, Keith . . . Keith . . . ? Dash it, old boy . . . where the deuce are you going?"

"For a bit of sport!" retorted Keith, vanishing behind the door.

Robby glared at the door in some indignation before breaking out into a verbose and violent diatribe on the dastardliness of being bullied out of one's sleep, set upon unmercifully, and then dropped without satisfactory explanation—all before the hour of seven in the morning. Really, this was the outside of enough!

The Marquess of Lyndhurst took the stairs much like a large cat tracking, every muscle working, stopping only when he was outdoors to survey his unfamiliar surroundings. Establishing the direction of the stables which he assumed were Miss Henshaw's destination, he hurried after her. At the stable door he caught his breath a moment before startling Jewelene with, "Why . . . Miss Henshaw?

This is wonderful indeed. It would appear that I am not alone in my passion for early morning excursions!"

Jewelene jumped and her almond-shaped eyes opened wide. He had the distinct sensation of falling into a deep green pool. She blushed, for her portmanteau was already secured on her saddled horse and in full view. There was no hiding it or the fact that she was not on any little morning excursion.

She had to think fast. She had no wish that he should go back to the house with a tale that would make her brother suspicious. Jimmy . . . she just couldn't let Jimmy know what she was about, for he would forbid it and then they —even Ben—would be undone. She managed a friendly smile in spite of her irritation. "Good morning, Mr. Robendale. What a surprise to find you up so early—but our mornings are most invigorating. If you are going to ride, I suggest you take the path through the west fields. There is a lovely view of the sea."

"Ah, but do *you* not ride?" he asked pointedly.

She rather squirmed before his persistence, and he felt a tingle of amusement. "Ride? Well . . . actually . . . it is not for pleasure that I ride this morning . . . I have an errand to discharge."

"Excellent. We can take to the road together. I can always view the sea . . . but your company, fair charmer, is far more to be treasured."

"How . . . gallant of you, sir . . . but . . ." she stammered for want of a ready excuse to throw him off.

"And in that manner you can teach me the way to town . . . as I shall be wanting to go there tonight," he added glibly.

"I . . . I did . . . not say I was going to town . . ." countered Jewelene, feeling the color rise in her cheeks.

"Oh? Are you not?"

She was irritated by his fine handling. Something in his persistence was beyond endurance, but still she maintained her composure. There was nothing for it but to surrender gracefully.

"Yes, sir, I am going to town . . . I have a parcel to drop off at a friend's house. You are most welcome to accompany me." She called back to the elderly groom awaiting instructions and had him saddle Keith's horse, saying lightly over her shoulder to the marquess, "I will just take my mare outdoors while your horse is being readied."

"I shall go with you," he said keeping in step.

He lounged against the stable wall and watched as she walked her horse by its leading string, conscious of her provocative form. Her hair, moving freely in the wind, fell to her waist—and her mind worked. He could tell, for her thoughts were almost betrayed by her eyes.

Jewelene watched him from beneath her lashes. His ginger hair blew about his lean, handsome face. His form was ridiculously arousing . . . absurd, she told herself, he was naught but a gambler. But then her father had been a gambler, and she knew her mother had never regretted a moment of her marriage.

She shot him another hasty look as his horse was brought out. He mounted and she felt a hint of admiration for the way he sat his horse. His shoulders were well laid back . . . yes, very handsome indeed, she thought, and then chastised herself, for there was little doubt that in all probability he was not only a penniless gamester but a rakehell too.

She mounted her mare without assistance and led the way to the front drive. The marquess managed his horse until he was riding abreast. He cast his eyes heavenward and spoke lightly.

"Sun seems to be trying."

"Hmmm . . . it always does this time of year, but no doubt it will rain," she responded in the same vein. Then suddenly, intently, she said, "Tell me, Mr. Robendale . . . I can understand your cousin's being here. He was probably given little choice. The dowager is a most strong-willed woman . . . very much in my heart, so don't think I mean to criticize . . . but you, sir, whatever are you doing here?"

"I told you last night, my dear. I am a gamester. At present one who is without a farthing to call his own. Robby is not only an excellent cousin but a most generous fellow as well. He has kept me out of dun territory in exchange for my company. You may wonder at his taste —but there it is," he said easily. He had prepared himself for just such a question and was in fact pleased that it had finally been asked.

"I see," she said sighing.

"Now, it is my turn, Miss Henshaw." His gray eyes were on her face.

"Whatever do you mean?"

"Have I not satisfied your curiosity on a point?" he asked.

"Well . . . yes . . . but . . ."

"I therefore require the same." His voice was smooth.

"Oh, very well . . . what is it?"

"How is it, Miss Henshaw, that you have not been snapped up?" he asked, coming directly to the point.

She laughed without mirth. "Oh, it was easy, I do assure you."

"Of course, I understand without a London Season it . . ." he started.

"Oh, but you mistake. I had a London Season when I was eighteen and my parents were . . . still alive," she corrected.

"Really . . . that would be . . . three years ago . . . that would explain how it came about that I did not see you. M'mother had a desire to see Boney defeated in '15 . . . we were in Brussels."

"Were you?" asked Jewelene. "Then you must have been there with the marquess and the dowager, for that is how we came to miss *them* during my Season."

The marquess felt very much like kicking himself. That could have been a near-fatal slip.

"Yes, we are a close-knit family, you see. But, Miss Henshaw, you quite astound me. A London Season . . . and yet you remained single. I cannot believe it is true. Did not your parents approve of any of the bucks that came courting?"

She dimpled. "How do you know any . . . bucks came courting?"

"You jest!" he answered jovially. "But truly . . ."

"Truly, sir, *I* did not approve," she answered simply.

"I see. And then, of course . . . there were the deaths of your parents . . ." he was musing aloud.

She looked rather shocked by his forwardness. "Mr. Robendale!"

"Oh, I am sorry! But you are no longer in mourning . . ."

"And I am also without a dowry," she answered curtly, feeling this was getting all too personal.

"It doesn't seem to bother Omsbury, but I imagine it would bother some of the *ton* . . ."

She was goaded into replying, "But not, I am relieved to see, the dowager or her son!" There was nothing sinister in her reply, but the marquess did not see it quite that way. He took up the challenge on Robby's behalf.

"Ah, of course . . . my cousin. But you are out there. Not that a dowry matters. Not at all, he couldn't give a fig about that, but he isn't in the petticoat line. Your cap would go unnoticed!"

"My . . . my . . . my . . . cap!" she blustered, fully irritated now and ready to do battle. "Let me tell you, sir. If I were to fling it his way . . . he would notice. Mark me! He would notice. The fact is I haven't put it in his way!"

"No, I rather fancy it lies in Omsbury's soil!" retorted the marquess irrationally.

She gasped, "How dare you?"

"I dare because I intend that you should cast all hopes of luring my cousin's heart for your own to the winds." He shouted, his voice searing her. His eyes gazed contemptuously over her wayward mode of attire, making her feel naked rather than fully dressed in her heavy buckskin jacket and breeches. "I take leave to tell you, Miss Henshaw, that you are a veritable spitfire, far too hot at hand, unbroke to bridle, and obviously unwilling to be, and far too unsuited for my gentle cousin!"

"Really?" she returned, her eyes of green ice cutting him. "How interesting an observation. We shall see, Mr. Robendale, I do promise you . . . we shall see!" She urged her horse into a canter.

He watched her spurt off on the mare, wanting to shake her, wanting to shake himself. How stupid he had been! The words had spilled out before he could stop himself. He had certainly blundered. He could see that. Robby had already admitted that he found the chit exciting. If she were to wage a full-scale attack . . . good God!

He spurred his horse forward and when they were once again abreast, he made an attempt to retrieve his position. "Miss Henshaw?"

She ignored him for her temper was flying about her head. He pursued softly, "Miss Henshaw?" and then again, "Miss Henshaw?" She reined in and rounded on him. "You are a . . . a . . . cad! How dare you speak to me in such a manner! If I were a man I would cut out your liver and feed it to Caesar!"

"Would you?" he said smiling at her. "How very bloodthirsty to be sure! But, Miss Henshaw. I do apologize."

She eyed him suspiciously, and her brows were still drawn together. "You hardly know me, yet you pronounced the most unflattering . . ."

Hastily he broke in before she planned further dissection of his person. "Please, Miss Henshaw . . . I retract them all. Only do not frown so, you will frighten off the sun!"

She glanced at him and because hers was a temper that never lasted long without fuel, she did allow him the favor of a curving mouth. He was struck by it and heartily glad he had made his retraction. If she were to let loose such a smile on poor unsuspecting Robby . . .

A few moments later they had reached the village square. Jewelene directed him to the local inn, and they agreed to meet there in thirty minutes. He stood back then and watched her cross the wide cobbled road to a narrow side street and then disappear from view. She certainly was a mystery, this Henshaw chit.

Six

His brows up, his eyes starting, Wailey stood aside and allowed Jewelene to enter. He had been about his duties the past twenty minutes and had much to do before the day officially began. Opening doors to would-be visitors at such an odd hour was not to his mind in keeping with the proprieties. But then Miss Henshaw was certainly quality, and he knew well what vagaries the quality could set about. He eyed her with some misgiving as she pushed her satchel into his hands and told him to stow it in the blue guest room abovestairs.

"But . . ."

"And not a word to Mrs. Clay. 'Tis Ben's orders. No one is to know. Understood?"

"Understood, but . . ."

"Mrs. Clay is still asleep, I hope?"

"I should say so, but . . ."

"Excellent. Don't wake Mr. Clay. I'll do that myself later. First, I've got to go up and talk to Lyla."

"But Miss Henshaw, Miss Lyla is still abed . . ."

"Wonderful!" said Jewelene mischievously, making for the narrow staircase. Wailey sighed and followed her up to deposit his charge.

Jewelene knew her way to Lyla's room without assistance. She moved in quickly, going straight to the windows and drawing the silk, straw-colored drapes aside. A sound came from the bed, something like a groan surely, and a rustle from the straw-colored silk quilts. "Who . . . what . . . ?" groaned a young woman's voice.

"Wake up, sleepy head," said Jewelene cheerily. She would have to tread warily if her plan was to succeed. Ben had warned her and she knew herself what Lyla was.

"Jewelene!" shrieked the girl from the bed, popping up to display a head of dark, closely cropped curls, large brown eyes, and a heart-shaped face. Small freckles added a touch of spice to the nose, one that was perhaps a shade too long for the small face. But the slightly petulant mouth gave one a total picture of a strikingly attractive creature. "Gracious! What are you doing here . . . at this hour . . . ?" Then as a thought struck her, "Huh! Ben, you have spent the night with Ben! Oh, Jewelene, you are ruined!"

"I certainly would be if I had done such a thing and then were foolish enough to allow *you* to discover it! Lud! It would be all over town within an hour's span! Stoopid girl!"

Lyla pouted, "Then what are you doing here?"

"I had to come without Jimmy, you see . . ."

"No, I don't—or perhaps I do. You don't like the fact that Jimmy is seeing so much of me, do you?"

"You know you are a dreadful little brat, and 'twould serve you if I left and did not give you a chance at the thing!" said Jewelene, artfully moving toward the door.

It was calculated, this remark, and it produced the desired result. Lyla jumped up from her quilts hastily. "Oh, Jewelene, don't pucker up now. Tell me do . . . why are you here?"

"As I was saying, it wouldn't do for Jimmy to know I was coming here to invite you to stay at Henshaw House!"

"What? But . . . why would Jimmy not like it? I imagine he would like it very well . . ." said Lyla putting her finger to her lip saucily and moving to and fro.

"Ho! Indeed he would . . . if the Marquess of Lyndhurst were not there!"

"Marquess . . . there is a marquess staying there?"

"Yes, and, of course, Jimmy would not want you thrown in his way . . . but then you see *I* would . . ." said Jewelene slowly.

"Why?" asked Lyla suspiciously.

"Two reasons! I don't wish to marry the marquess. I am not really interested . . ."

"I know. You care naught for money and a title. Anyway I have always thought you were more than half in love with Ben! I don't know why you deny it!"

Jewelene felt very much like tearing out her hair, but she calmed herself and continued. "At any rate . . ."

Lyla interrupted her. "Still . . . it doesn't explain. If you don't want the marquess for yourself, why then not for Elizabeth?"

"Elizabeth does not seem to be in his style, and to be frank . . . one doesn't quite want to lose a marquess . . ."

"Why don't you be really honest? You are afraid I will steal your precious Sir James before he is breeched and would rather I took up with this marquess of yours!"

"I don't suppose it would do any good to deny it. So, very well. Do you wish to come have a go at it?"

"Indeed I do. I shall have Ben drive me over this afternoon with my things."

"Ta-ta, Lyla . . ." said Jewelene, going to the door.

She was at Ben's door a moment later knocking softly. He was expecting her and came out in his dressing gown. "Don't give me any of your good mornings." he said curtly, leading her downstairs. "I was up till all hours playing piquet against Omsbury, and I'm dead . . ."

"Never say you lost?" cried Jewelene, turning on her heel, her eyes searching his face.

He smiled. "You must learn not to interrupt. I was about to say I am dead on my feet and, no, I did not lose, but I didn't win enough either. It took me nearly all night to win but 300 pounds. I still owe the devil . . . never mind . . ."

"You still owe him 4700 pounds," Jewelene finished dismally.

He closed the parlor door behind them and stared hard at her. "How the deuce did you know that?"

"Omsbury paid me a little visit . . . last night. He told me you had lost personally to him 5000 . . . oh, 'tis all my fault. You did it for us . . ."

"Nonsense! Now tell me, did you arrange it with Lyla?"

"Yes, she comes to us this afternoon. Now we have only to make certain that, when you let me in at night, Mrs. Clay is out of the way."

"Don't worry, m'mother always retires by nine to her rooms," he said.

"Then it is all settled. Oh, Ben, I am so excited. I must do well . . . and, Ben, I intend to engage Omsbury in a game of piquet myself!" she said purposefully.

"You will do no such thing!"

"I will promise not to . . . if you give me the same oath," she offered.

He looked at her and flicked her nose. "You are a sly rogue."

"And I will make the house enough money to kick Omsbury in the . . ."

"Never mind! Off with you!" he said, laughing.

"See you this afternoon then."

"Yes. I suppose everyone will be there . . ." said Ben hesitatingly.

Jewelene smiled. "Indeed . . . so look your best!"

At the White Stag the marquess became engrossed with two gentlemen who had arrived some few minutes after him in search of a room. It appeared there was a pugilism match scheduled during the week, and nearly every inn on Wight was completely booked. They were in high spirits and the marquess was enjoying a hearty round of exchanges when Jewelene sauntered into the public galley.

The fair young gentleman on the marquess's right put down his pewter of coffee and stared hard before nudging the marquess.

"By Jove! Look at that rough-and-tumble piece! Every inch of her made for tossing!"

Keith's gray eyes hardened and, for no particular reason, he felt very much like landing his new friend a facer and taking Jewelene over his knee. He said curtly, "Excuse me, gentlemen!" and marched across the room to intercept her entrance. Roughly he took her by the arms and steered her forcibly round toward the exit.

"What do you think you are doing?" she gasped incredulously, trying to disengage his hold.

He was furious. After all he owed it to Mrs. Debbs to protect her niece from making a cake of herself. He owed it to his mother who seemed to like the chit. He owed it to . . . damnation! He owed it to her for she was something of a hoyden and needed schooling. "Devil is in it, Miss Henshaw, I am doing what is necessary! Have you no sense walking into a public galley dressed as you are, inviting insult to yourself?"

Jewelene blushed. Indeed, she had not thought. She was

so used to going about with her brother, having his protection, that it just did not occur to her that she would be seriously breaching the proprieties by sauntering into the tavern room. However, her defenses were up, and her green eyes sparked at him. "How the deuce was I to tell you I was ready to go home? Surely you didn't expect me to stand about outside?"

"I expected you to send word to me. That is what those link boys out there are for!" he snapped.

She bit her lip and went to her horse in defiant silence. Mounting, she started onto the road ahead of him. He paid the link boys for their service, took up his reins, mounted, and followed in her wake. At length he led his horse into a canter and gathered ground, bringing himself abreast. "I seem to remember, Miss Henshaw, a promise to give me a tour of Yarmouth Castle."

She glanced sidewise at him. "It doesn't open until later. I inquired on my way to the inn. Perhaps Jimmy will do it another time."

"The promise came from *you*, and I expect you to keep it," he said uncompromisingly.

"Very well, but you shan't enjoy it!" she threatened.

"That is probably true," he bantered.

She eyed him but decided to remain silent. He sighed, "Do you always torture those who find disfavor in your eyes?"

"Always! I am most spiteful!" she answered coldly. "In addition to having no sense, being hot at hand—and what else did you dub one of my traits? . . . oh, yes, unbridled!"

"Ah, and there is yet another thing I have discovered about you," he sallied. "You hold a grudge!"

"Horrid man! I do not!"

"But you forgave me my trespasses earlier, and here you are raking them up!"

She blushed. "I think, sir, that I find you . . . detestable and disagreeable."

"It stands to reason, of course," he answered blandly.

"What does?"

"That if you find me detestable, you must then find me disagreeable." He was smiling and in spite of herself she smiled in return.

"Odious fellow . . . you are rude!" But she was smiling.

"Why? Because of my lamentable habit of speaking the truth?"

"Because you speak your mind, it does not automatically follow you are speaking the truth, sir," she countered.

"*Touché!* Now am I forgiven?"

"For a time, I suppose, for a time. Oh, I am ravenous! Are you?"

He looked at her face, and his eyes wandered to the full breasts beneath the white linen shirt and buckskin jacket. His eyes went to her lips, and he said in his most provocative manner, "Extremely so, Miss Henshaw."

She blushed furiously for his meaning was not lost on her, and she felt an absurd flush of pleasure steal over her. Averting her face she urged her horse into a faster gait. The marquess smiled to himself. She was not immune to his charms. He was nearly certain of it, but she gave him no invitation. Why not? Because she thought him titleless and penniless! What would she do if she knew . . . how would she smile? For an instant he wished she did know, but he banished such weakness the moment it dared to raise its head.

Seven

"But Jewelene . . . dearest . . . how could you?" ejaculated Aunt Dora, much distraught. She gestured imploringly. "Why . . . why invite Lyla Clay at such a time?"

"She won't be any bother to you, Aunt Dora, and really it would so help Mrs. Clay's jangled nerves to have Lyla stay with us for a time."

"But . . . but . . . the marquess . . . you . . . Elizabeth . . ." floundered Mrs. Debbs, feeling very much as though she were about to have a spasm. Really, it was bad enough with neither Jewelene nor Elizabeth making a push to engage the marquess's interest, but then to bring in such competition—why it was beyond everything intolerable.

Jewelene was well aware of her aunt's feelings, and she was not without pity. She patted Aunt Dora's agitated hand soothingly. "Dear Aunt, you are so good to care . . . but don't you see? I could not, *would* not, marry the Marquess of Lyndhurst if he were to break down my door and declare himself my suitor. I . . . I like him well enough . . . but not in *that* way."

"But you scarcely know him," objected her aunt. "How do you know that in time . . ."

"Because I know," she answered gravely.

"And what of your duty to your cousin? If you will not take him yourself, why then do you cloud the road for Elizabeth?"

Jewelene gave a short laugh. It was so absurd, speaking in this manner as though the marquess were some heaven-sent treasure to be scooped up at all costs. "Oh, Aunt

Dora . . . I am surprised at you. How can you put Elizabeth in such light? How can you possibly think Lyla competition for Liz? If the marquess had any organization in his upper works, he could never choose Lyla over Liz! If he could, then he wouldn't be worth the having, let me tell you!"

"But, but . . ."

"Ah . . . I do believe I hear a carriage coming now . . ." said Jewelene, jumping up. She went to the window and her aunt glanced over her. She was certainly looking a beauty in her blue muslin print, her honey tresses gleaming all about her delicate shoulders in that most fetching way. One thing was certain, if the marquess had any eyes, he should fall madly in love with her, but she was less sure about her own daughter.

Jewelene wrapped her ivory knit shawl about her and skipped out of the room, stopping on her way at the dining room where Elizabeth was working with the flower arrangements. "Liz . . . Liz . . . come with me, do, for Aunt is determined to snub Lyla, and I need your support!" There was a strange light in Jewelene's eye, but Elizabeth seemed too engrossed in her flowers to notice it.

Jewelene cast an appraising glance at Elizabeth. She was quite fetching in her dove-colored muslin, and a soft rosiness suffused her cheeks. Jewelene had seen Elizabeth conversing with the marquess earlier and wondered now about it. Could she be attracted to the plump nobleman? Well, he was certainly a sweet sort . . . perhaps she was. "Here," she said, picking up Elizabeth's shawl and handing it to her, "wear this, it's chilly outdoors today. Now come along."

Elizabeth laughed and Jewelene couldn't help notice that there was a glow on her countenance and a softness in her fawnlike eyes that had not been there yesterday. "You know, Lizzie, my pet," she said softly, "you are a beauty . . . indeed you are!"

Elizabeth blushed and linked her arm through her cousin's. "Nonsense. You are just prejudiced by love."

The real Marquess of Lyndhurst and his cousin emerged from the stables, pausing for a moment to allow Sir James to catch up to them. They had ridden out to the training pen to watch Lightning perform and were absorbed in their discussion regarding the horse's chances. However the sound of carriage wheels made them turn their heads, and Sir James's smile widened when he saw who was coming upon them.

"Ben! Lyla? Why, this is famous! Do you come to lunch? I didn't know. My dratted sister forgot to inform me."

Keith watched the greeting between Ben Clay and Sir James. He noted the military cut of Ben's well-fitting coat, the shine of his hessians, the attractiveness of his countenance, and the empty sleeve. He frowned, curious, before his eyes then found Lyla Clay. She was smiling invitingly at him and at Robby.

"James . . . you must introduce us to your friends," she said audaciously.

Her brother frowned at her but Jimmy came quickly to the fore and did the thing neatly and without ceremony. "Come on," he added, "leave your carriage here. Our man can see to it and you can walk. Look, here come Liz and Jewel to bear us company!"

Ben jumped down easily—he had long ago learned the trick of such maneuvering—and he turned to aid his sister before relinquishing her company. Indeed, she gave him little choice. She eyed Keith flirtatiously but fell in step beside Robby, showering him with as many charms as possible. Keith sized her up in a moment as vulgar and turned to walk with Sir James and Ben Clay.

Jewelene and her cousin reached them somewhat breathlessly; Keith stood back and watched with interest as she put an arm about Ben's waist and stood on tiptoe to kiss his cheek. Pretty familiar with him, he thought to himself, with a twinge of something he could not identify.

"Ah, Ben, I am so pleased . . . you do remember Elizabeth . . ." she said, turning to include her cousin.

"Of course," said Ben promptly, his eyes meeting with Liz's. "It is a pleasure to see you again, Miss Debbs."

"Thank you, Mr. Clay," said Liz quietly, "shall we go in?" She was looking at Lyla and Robby and then turned toward the house. Jewelene watched and wondered what was happening, if anything.

"Yes, do, all of you go in. Aunt Dora is waiting in the parlor," agreed Jewelene, holding Ben's gloved hand, detaining him so that Elizabeth found herself beside Keith. The marquess felt another twinge, but this time he knew it was annoyance that plagued him. Why? Because he was curious, he told himself, and she was so damnably mysterious.

Ben stood back and watched Elizabeth go off on Keith's arm and his sister on Robby's, with Sir James doing circles round his guests in order to be a part of the conversation. Then he frowned. "What now, puss?"

"I received a note from Omsbury earlier. I didn't show it to James, but . . . oh Ben, we shall have to do something soon."

"Let me see it!"

She took it from her boot and put it in his hands. He glanced down to read:

Jewelene,
    You have another week in which to make up your mind to it. I want you and can no longer wait. I hold several notes over your friend Clay's head. They all fall due in less than two weeks!
    To put it delicately, he could lose everything he has. Could—but, of course, need not. It will depend on my mood two weeks hence.
                       Your obedient,
                        Omsbury

Ben crushed the note in his hand, and his expression was violent. "Villain! I'll have his neck for this!"

"Now, Ben . . ." she said, placing a restraining hand on his arm, for he appeared to have every intention of carrying out his threat immediately.

"Nay . . . it won't serve! We shall have to come up with the money."

He stopped, his mouth drawn into a sneer. "Yes, and then I will run him through!"

"Oh, Ben, I wish you may, but first the money. But we will talk more about it later," she added, for she could see that both her brother and Mr. Keith Robendale were at the bay window watching them. "Come, they will be wondering what we are about!"

Inside, Lyla glanced out the window and tittered. "Oh, my, I don't know why they just don't name the day! La, but anyone can see they're in love!"

"You have no notion what you are talking about!" snapped Mrs. Debbs, wishing very much that Jewelene would come in and not give Lyla room for such sport.

However, it appeared that only Mr. Robendale seemed curious over Lyla's statement. The marquess seemed more interested in the appetizers.

Mrs. Debbs then glanced at her daughter whose sparkle of the morning seemed somehow to have faded. Oh, gracious! Was Liz upset over Lyla's vulgar flirting with the marquess? Why then did she not make herself more agreeable to him? No, she would only take a back seat. . . .

The parlor door opened, and Jewelene and Ben Clay came gliding in. Sir James beamed upon them, "Good, you are in time to settle a question, Ben!"

"Eh? What is that?"

"Not now!" said Mrs. Debbs, eager to get everyone into the dining room. She had the seating arrangements just so. "I am quite certain we are all famished. Come along, children, come along."

Ben shrugged his shoulders and, as he was standing near Elizabeth, he offered her his arm. She blushed and accepted, as Sir James led the way with his aunt. Lyla had already attached herself to the marquess and thus it was that Keith turned a mocking smile to Jewelene. "Miss Henshaw?" he said, offering her his arm.

She cast him a saucy look and accepted his offer, noting that to touch him was strangely uncomfortable. She felt a warmth throughout her body and knew that she was blushing. Idiot! she told herself, lifting her chin.

Eight

A raven-haired siren stood in Ben's richly furnished apartment on the second floor of his three-story establishment known to the gamesters of Wight as the Silver Heart. He took a step backward, his hand cupping his chin, and eyed her critically. A bright natural hair wig covered her own tawny locks. Thick clusters of Grecian curls were arranged all about her head and fell down upon bare white shoulders. Patches were no longer à la mode, but she had chosen to affix one, heart-shaped, just above her curving cherry lips, and the effect was charming. A black, pointed satin mask curved over her eyes, the slits permitting only their green glints to show through. The gown held an old world quality and was obviously not designed for a maid. Of red satin, it was cut most daringly and fell in a clinging fashion about her figure. The long train was beaded with jet, and a bracelet of the same stones attached the folds to Jewelene's wrist. Her hands were ungloved.

Ben watched her as she whirled round, and indeed she did not look herself, but some French beauty stepping forth from the stage. Not at all respectable but most bewitching! He gave a soft whistle, "Lord, woman, you will do! Far too well, I suspect!" He shook his head as though somewhat bothered. "I hope you are prepared to hear the most outrageous proposals . . . for you will hear them, m'girl! Mark me . . . you will certainly hear them!"

"Oh, yes, I know, Ben, but do not fret it, love, they won't be making them to me, will they? They will be propositioning . . . BABETTE! So we mustn't take insult, must we?" She was teasing but cautioning as well.

"Aye, but I don't like it, puss. I mean, it isn't as though you were some . . . I mean, you are a Henshaw!"

"Oh, Ben, don't worry, really." She tilted her head and put on her accent, "Oh, you staid English do worry. Zees eez naught, I do you assure . . ."

He smiled indulgently. "Well, m'girl, you had better carry it off or our heads will roll—together!"

"I shall, Ben, I promise you."

"There is another thing that worries me . . . your riding home at night alone . . ."

She snapped her fingers in the air. " 'Tis naught!"

"Well, I won't have it. I've made up my mind to it. I'll have Silas watch the E.O. table for me, and I'll take you home m'self."

"Ben, that is silly . . ." she objected.

"You agree to it, m'girl, or you don't walk from this room!" he threatened.

"Oh," she sighed resignedly, "very well . . ." and, patting his hand, preceded him out of the room.

Patrons of the Silver Heart had already begun to arrive, and Jewelene could hear their jovial voices below. A ruddy individual of some size and foreboding mien stood at the door of the first-floor entrance. He was Angus, and there wasn't an upstart, bruiser, or rum touch that could get past his knowing eye. For the regulars of his master's exclusive gaming house he had a ready smile, for the newly initiated a penetrating gaze, and for his master's intimates, a private jest or two. And there wasn't a man who passed the Silver Heart's portals who didn't wish to have Angus's approval.

Soon the first-floor hall was filled with sounds of merriment, and Jewelene could hear them making their way to the second floor where the gaming rooms were situated. Ben eyed her a moment as he went about his business. After all, this would certainly be an ordeal for his little Jewel—whether she would admit it or not. But he could see that she was bearing up, steady as ever.

He would have been very much more concerned had he known her heart at that moment. Jewelene's pulse beat at an extraordinary rate. Really, girl, she told herself, playing faro with Ben and papa and beating them is not quite the same as dealing at a gaming house. You are good—but are you good enough to win for the house against all the men who will be arriving night after night? Good Lord . . . *here they come!*

"Egad!" ejaculated one happy young man as he entered the room and discovered at the head of the faro table a mysterious, raven-haired beauty. "Egad, I say!"

The gentleman at his side immediately put up a gold-rimmed quizzing glass and then dropped it carelessly so that it swung on its dark riband. "I surrender!" he offered, forgetting his companion and going forward to display his intentions. "Take me . . ." he said, going down on one knee and reaching for Jewelene's hand.

She pulled her hand away with a laugh. *"Mais non,* m'sieur, get up, do . . ."

"If it is your wish," offered the gallant, "but tell me what I may do to please you, and I shall contrive to do it immediately!"

"Ah, *mais oui,* that is easy. You will lose at my faro table, *oui?*" smiled Jewelene naughtily.

"Done!" replied the gallant.

His friend had by this time arrived on the scene. "He can't lose half as much as I!"

Jewelene put up her hands. "Gentlemen, gentlemen... come sit on either side of me, and I shall contrive to take as much as you are willing to lose..."

They were entranced. Her accent was perfect, her dark hair, her mask, everything about her was bewitching, and it was not long before Jewelene's table was overflowing.

It was some time later that Jewelene looked up from her table and felt her heart flutter. Oh, no! Good God! She should have been prepared . . . after all he had said he was a gambler. For there coming purposefully towards her was the marquess's handsome cousin, Keith Robendale. A slight smile curved his sensuous mouth and his gray eyes glittered. Drat! Drat, and drat again! thought Jewelene. I mean . . . it was one thing to tip a rise to men she had never before met in her entire life and would just as lief never meet again, and quite another thing to accomplish her task with a man who was now a guest in her home. She would have to be careful.

Ben saw Keith and turned quickly to his "lookout" man, Silas. Silas watched the bets at the E.O. table, collected the winnings for the house after each spin of the wheel, or paid them out. "Take over for me, Silas, have Jem watch," he whispered as he moved away and hastened to intercept the marquess's dashing cousin.

"Robendale," he called heartily. "How good of you to come by."

Keith turned his attention from the raven-haired beauty and smiled amiably. "If I had known that you had such a creature dealing your faro table, I assure you, sir, I would have come long ago!"

"Oh? Is faro your game?" asked Ben trying to steer the conversation, and hopefully the gentleman, away from his object.

"As to that, 'tis écarté that holds my interest . . ." started Keith.

"Écarté! Well then, my friend, you are in luck. We have a game in the chamber across the hall. I believe there is already a spectator bet going on but plenty of room for another . . . shall I take you in?"

Keith glanced towards the masked lovely. "Perhaps later . . . for the moment . . . I think I'll try my luck at faro."

Ben's eyes flickered, and this was not lost on the marquess.

"Very well then, Mr. Robendale . . . but I give you fair warning, our Babette is really a wonder. Her skill with the cards is such that our house has done up most of those poor fellows there."

"The wonder, my friend, is that those . . . er . . . poor fellows can lose and still look so well pleased," replied the marquess drily. He moved away slowly to Jewelene's side. She glanced up and gave him a bright smile in spite of her agitation. Audaciously he inclined his head toward her, nearly touching her shoulder as he brought his eyes up to meet her own through the mask.

She glanced away hurriedly. "Place your bets, messieurs . . ."

"I see there is no sitting room, mamselle . . . would you mind if I took up position here?"

"*Mais non,* eet eez impossseeble, m'sieur. You leave me . . . so tight." She glanced at one of her worshipers. "Ah, Filey . . . make room, *chéri* . . ." She turned her eyes to the marquess. "There, m'sieur . . . you may squeeze in, *oui?*"

The marquess had not become a deft flirt without knowing when to launch his assault and when to retreat. He withdrew his line of attack with excellent grace and allowed the French beauty to position him. This he found not altogether without its merits. From his new stance he was quite able to get an excellent view of the lady's many charms, and every now and then was able to catch her eyes . . . and such eyes! They were made, or so it seemed to him, of green glitter, if only he could see their framework. It would be his objective to unmask this belle, for there was no denying that he did not intend his sojourn in the country to make a monk of him.

"La, Filey . . ." laughed the lady coquettishly, "do not fight with your good friend. You and Hill may both take me to zee suppair . . . *oui?*"

"No!" said Filey vehemently. "Why must *he* come?" asked the young man referring to the gentleman who until tonight had been his closest friend.

Jewelene chuckled, but she was not given the opportunity to respond to this, for suddenly, and with an expertise that certainly deserved applause, she found herself taken up by the dashing ginger-haired blade known to her as Keith Robendale. He scarcely gave the indignant younger men a second glance as he said eloquently, "My trump, lads," and led the masked beauty away.

Jewelene was unable to speak, did not in fact trust herself to do so. She had to be careful . . . she had to maintain her accent. If she were to lose her temper she must do so in French. She decided to try to keep silent.

The marquess said after a moment, "You know your game well, mamselle. Have you been dealing faro at the Silver Heart long?"

"No, m'sieur. Tonight . . . she is my first . . ." she said in a small voice, averting her eyes, wishing he would not look so closely at her.

"My compliments to you, mamselle. Not only have you won for the house, but you have done so for yourself as well," he said somewhat drily.

"Your meaning, m'sieur?"

"One cannot deny the conquests you have made," he answered, somewhat surprised at her lack of understanding and wondering if she were perhaps trying to beguile him.

She said nothing to this, and he frowned again, "Why the mask, my pretty?"

"Ah . . . but you seem . . . 'ow do you Englishmen say it . . . ah, *oui*, up to every rig . . .? So . . . 'ow then you do not 'ave zee answer?" she said, dipping deeply into her accent.

He laughed shortly but pursued. "Enlighten me, if you will please, for though I have always considered myself . . . er . . . up to every rig, I have not yet found a rational reason for covering up such beauty as you evidently possess!"

"Ah . . . but I may be quite ordinary. Eet eez posseeble . . . *n'est-ce pas?*" she countered.

"No, you have not covered up . . . quite enough to make anyone believe that fustian!"

She laughed. "Very well, m'sieur . . . you insist on my secret, I give eet to you. You have said I made conquests, *oui?*"

"Yes . . . but . . ."

She interrupted him. "No, no, I do not mind. *Moi*, I am pleased with eet, but perhaps I want more. And would *you* not agree that zair ees something beguiling . . . intriguing . . . about mystery?"

He looked at her full, and the corner of his mouth moved almost imperceptibly, "Ah, I begin to see."

"*Oui*, zat eez good. For one understands that a lovely woman in . . . such a place . . . can be found. Eet eez not so very difficult. She makes a hit . . . *oui*, but then, she eez no longer zee rage. . . . Ah, but a lady in a mask whose identity is unknown . . . ah, m'sieur, I think such a woman would hold the stage . . . *oui?*"

"And that is what you wish to do . . . hold the stage?" he asked curiously, stopping her ever so gently so that they faced each other at the top of the ornate staircase.

Jewelene looked him full in the face. She was being brazen, audacious, she was playing a part, but oh, God! if it were ever discovered who she really was, she would be ruined. But she had to continue with it, for it was the only way she could keep herself, already somewhat in the mire, from being discovered. She must be Babette, and Babette would say, "But, of course, m'sieur . . . what else eez zair?"

"I could, my pretty, think of yet another setting for you . . ." he ventured, his ungloved hand going to her chin.

He quite took her breath away, but she was outraged in spite of Ben's earlier warnings. Ben had said she would receive just such a proposal . . . but really it was very hard not to retort, it was very hard to keep her hand from raking a vicious path across his rugged cheek. Her eyes glittered with anger, but her voice belied it. "I think, m'sieur," she said slowly, "that the lobster salad is reported to be quite delicious."

He had not missed the furious glare of her eyes. It had surprised him. After all, a hellcat . . . a gaming wench . . . must be quite used to such things, and he had put it more delicately than most of his kind would have been apt to do. However, he allowed her affront to go unheeded and smiled, "Indeed my raven . . ."

"Keith!" ejaculated a plump young man from the hall below. "Get your hands off me, you oafish brute . . . Keith . . . !" shouted Robby.

The marquess gazed down to find his cousin near to fisticuffs with Angus at the entrance. He chuckled deeply as he led Babette to the scene.

"Keith . . . thank God! This . . . clunch meant to keep me out . . ."

Keith laughed. "You had but to show him your card, Robby . . ."

"Couldn't do that . . ." hissed Robby, "you've got m'cards . . . remember . . ."

His cousin frowned, remembering all too well. "Yes. . . but didn't you have the set I gave you?"

"No . . . forget 'em . . . look . . . just tell this daft creature that I ain't no skirter . . ."

"Indeed, Angus," said a deep voice at their backs. "You are detaining the Marquess of Lyndhurst."

They all turned to find Ben making his way towards them. He offered his outstretched hand to Robby with an apologetic smile. "I am sorry, my lord, but Angus does have strict orders not to let anyone pass unless he has been identified. It usually saves us a great deal of trouble."

"Humph!" said Robby, not at all mollified. "The thing is . . . do I look like a rum'un . . . I mean, really!"

Robby then found four pair of eyes critically surveying him and rudely remembered that he was in no fit state to be appraised. On the short ride from the tavern at the other end of town where he had been enjoying good company and good ale he had sustained something of a riding accident. Much in his cups, and feeling fit, he took the road somewhat haphazardly, landing his horse in a rut, stumbling the poor prime blood, and taking something of a fall himself. This left him rather bruised and his clothes somewhat less than perfect.

"Well, fiend seize it, Rob, you ain't as smart as when I left you! What in thunder happened to you?"

Robby glanced down at his clothing, then at the masked beauty before him, and flushed, "Not now. Look, if everyone is satisfied I'm no commoner, I'll take m'self off for a bit of freshening up."

Ben smiled gently and took up Robby's arm. "Certainly, old man, I'll lead the way." He stopped and touched Jewelene's hand and looked her full in the face, "Well, love . . . I shan't be long."

This too was not lost on Keith, Marquess of Lyndhurst, but when his penetrating glance once again rested on Jewelene's face, it was with much surprise to find her blushing furiously.

Nine

It was past three in the morning when Jewelene was finally able to close down the faro table. Hurriedly she had changed in Ben's home, and then together they had slipped away. Their movements went unnoticed, and they were able to get their horses without hindrance. The excitement of it all as they cantered across the fields engendered a wild laugh in them both, and they stopped for a moment to regain their poise.

"Dash it, girl!" apostrophized Ben amiably, "you are an incorrigible hoyden!" He sighed as the chuckles were replaced with quiet. "You put me much in mind of your father."

"Yes, I am every bit his child . . . but admit it you horrid man, you have enjoyed this night's work!" bantered Jewelene.

He gazed at her a long moment. Her tawny gold locks were wild about her lovely head. Yes, he had enjoyed outwitting everyone tonight. He hadn't been this charged since his days in Spain. But, he owed Jewelene's father a sight more than risking her to such sport. It worried him, and so he frowned.

She saw it and countered, "Lud! By that sour face, m'bucko, anyone would think the house had lost that five hundred tonight instead of winning it! I did well. Admit it, you fiend, I did well!"

He smiled ruefully, "Yes, your table did very well but . . ."

"No, Ben! I shan't let you bring me down! We came off

with it. Why even the marquess and his cousin did not know me."

"That's the rub! I mean really, Jewel . . . they will no doubt be dropping by quite often . . . and what with seeing you during the day and then Babette at night . . ."

"Pooh! Babette and Jewelene have naught in common. They will not guess. Now, sweet friend, take yourself off . . ."

"Hold there, m'girl . . ." he started to interrupt her.

"Don't," she interupted, "tell me you mean to see me to my door, Ben." There was a naughty look in her eyes. "Especially when I have told you I don't mean to be using any doors."

He laughed in spite of himself. They were on Henshaw land and although he couldn't make out the outline of the stables, he knew they were close at hand. "Very well, get thee home, minx!"

She clucked softly and urged her horse forward. He watched her vanish into the darkness. She was something, was his Jewelene. Rough and tumble, headstrong, and though a beauty, she had ever been too wilful to be in his style. But all the same she was as dear to him, perhaps dearer, than his own sister. He could not like this game they were at. As her friend he should not have allowed her to ride roughshod over him. He should have taken the reins, but dammit! the chit was pluck to the backbone. He knew if he hadn't lent his hand in this she would have done something equally dangerous on her own. Better that he was in on it to help should she tumble. He sighed and turned his horse back towards Yarmouth.

"You were cool as a cucumber, old boy." said Robby, leaning forward in his saddle to adjust his seat. "You dropped money on that faro table tonight without blinking your eye. Should have come to bet on that écarté game in the other room. Came off myself with a few coins," said he proudly.

"Think I begrudge a few guineas when I'm after game?" said the marquess, his thin lips curling.

"Eh? Oh, the masked chit? They could talk of naught else. There wasn't a man there tonight who don't have intentions in that direction. But I think you will all be out!" he said with the air of great confidence.

The marquess smiled patronizingly. "Really, Rob? What makes you say so?"

"Now, Keith, don't come off the Grand Turk to me!" countered Robby immediately. "Just thought you shouldn't waste your time."

"Don't be a lobcock. She may be a hellcat, but good Lord, Rob, didn't you get a look at her? She is worth every effort!"

"As to looking at her, I did . . . but that don't make any odds!" sighed Robby. "I was trying to tell you that the chit is already owned!"

"What?" snapped Keith, his head going round to eye his cousin dubiously. "Well come on, out with it!"

"No need to fratch at me, Keith. But I did happen to see her go into that fellow Clay's office and when they left . . . *they left together*. At least I think it was her . . . she was all wrapped up in some dark cloak. And then they were gone, almost as though they hadn't been there at all, but they were . . . had to be her with him . . . stands to reason . . ."

Keith was frowning, "Why does it stand to reason?"

"Told you. Saw Babette go into Clay's office, then went off m'self to get a glass of the bubbly. When I passed by again, I saw Clay with his arm about her . . . they were just slipping down the hall. Turned m'head for a moment at something that young Filey said and when I looked again, they were gone, just like that—poof!" he said, snapping his fingers for emphasis.

"How do you know it was Babette with Clay? You said yourself she was cloaked," pursued the marquess.

"Aye, just thought it was . . ."

"But you could be wrong?"

"Could be . . ." said Robby, but doubtfully.

"At any rate . . ." then as something ahead caught his eye he hissed, "Look there!"

Robby followed the line of the marquess's hand and noted a lone male rider some distance from them. He shot his cousin a repressive look.

"What's to do? After all, 'tis just some chap probably on his way home."

Ben Clay had been riding down the post road, it was safer than sticking to the fields where he might catch his horse in a rabbit hole. But now, observing the two riders coming toward him, he chided himself for a dunce. He couldn't be certain, but in all probability the two riders coming this way were the marquess and his cousin. There was but one thing to do. He took the fence flying and vanished into the field.

The marquess had halted his horse, his brows drawn, his eyes trying to penetrate the dark. He had seen the lone rider, and there was something familiar about the man's form. And then the fellow was up and over the field fence, and he had no doubt whatsoever it was Ben Clay. He had seen the folded empty sleeve as the cloak flew backwards during the jump. "Odd . . . there is something very odd about all this," he thought to himself. "Why . . . why would Ben Clay be out here at this hour? And why would he wish to avoid detection?"

"Was that Ben Clay?" asked Robby in surprise. "Couldn't make out his face myself."

"It was," replied the marquess thoughtfully.

"See? It's as I told you. He was taking his gaming wench home," said Robby with an air of satisfaction.

"Clunch!" said the marquess, "that is unlikely. Other than the Henshaw estate there are very few houses about."

"Oh, I don't know. I know there are a few side roads . . . may lead to farmhouses and such . . ." offered Robby.

"Babette—a farmer's daughter?" scoffed the marquess.

"Well then . . . he was visiting his sister. . . ."

"Dolt! At nearly four in the morning?"

"Well, then, nothing for it, Keith. He must have a nice little cottage here about where he keeps his French chit!"

The marquess paid little heed to this, saying only—and more to himself than to his cousin, "There is something smoky afoot. Why does the chit wear a mask? Why keep her out here . . . so far from his own snug bed if she is indeed his paramour?"

Robby searched his brain for an answer to this and, discovering the task beyond his capabilities, emitted an exasperated sigh.

"You know, Keith, it is as I said. Shouldn't have come to this isle . . . strange place, queer sorts. I mean . . . French chits sporting masks . . . fellows riding about the countryside at four in the morning. House full of ladies . . . that Lyla, you know . . . followed me about with her chatter till I was near to losing m'mind. Think we should throw in our towels and get back to London! Tell your mother it didn't take."

"But, Robby, how poor spirited of you! Quit? Now, dash it, old boy! It has just begun to get interesting, this sojourn of ours. No, I think we will play it out."

"Had this uncomfortable feeling you were going to say something like that," sighed Robby.

Clothed in a bright yellow muslin and carrying a large, old, and much worn portmanteau Jewelene sped down the hall from the rear third-floor staircase to her room. She closed her door and breathed a sigh of relief. "Whew! That was close!" she told Caesar who had chosen to take a nap beside her fireplace. "I thought Aunt Dora was going to come upon me for certain. Thank the Lord, she went to Elizabeth's call. I wonder what is afoot?" she sighed and put down the portmanteau on the bed. She had spent much of the morning in the attic retrieving the best of her mother's gowns. Only two would do for her purpose. She fervently hoped that Ben would come for a visit. She wanted to put them in his hands for they needed airing out, and she certainly could not do that with everyone about. These particular gowns had been made for her mother just before her death. They were still quite fresh and lovely, but Jewelene knew that she would be unable to claim that she wanted them for herself.

She stuffed the bag with the gowns and its accessories beneath her bed. Caesar, watching all this, thumped his tail for it appeared that his mistress was in the mood for play. However, she was quick to understand and repressed him immediately.

"Oh, no! You are *not* to touch! Understand?" she said firmly.

He looked askance at her but her tone was clearly one he recognized. He was not certain what he was not to do and therefore remained where he was, his tongue dangling sidewise and his tail beating the floor.

She sighed and put a finger to her mouth. Her thoughts were many and her canine seemed a willing audience. "Well, I don't think this is half as much fun as I imagined it would be. For one thing, Caesar, I dislike deceiving Aunt Dora. But you will admit we are in dire straits, and I can't put the problem on young Jimmy's head."

Caesar gave a lusty sigh and dropped his head to his paws, evidently much in sympathy with his mistress. Jewelene turned to her mirror. As she brushed her long hair her thoughts reverted to the previous evening. It had been a frightening experience in spite of all her bravado. The compliments she had received were far bolder than she had expected, and she had at first been quite shocked. Then her ordeal with the marquess and his wild cousin . . . that had really agitated her.

The thought that she would now have to meet them again did nothing to allay her concern. She had overslept this morning and missed seeing them at breakfast. Then her search in the attic had kept her safely out of reach, but there was nothing for it now, she would just have to go down and face them. She picked up her lightweight spencer and making her way to the door, turned to invite Caesar to join her.

"Come along, brute, Jimmy will be wanting you, no doubt."

Belowstairs in the parlor were Elizabeth, Lyla Clay, Keith, and Robby. They had been conversing for some twenty minutes when Mrs. Debbs left them on some errand.

Keith found himself studying Elizabeth and then engaged her in conversation, all the while laughing to himself to see Lyla fawning over poor Robby.

"It would appear we are not to see your cousins this morning," he remarked lightly after exhausting all the chitchat he could bring to mind and deciding that Elizabeth was a very poor conversationalist.

"Oh, I believe Sir James is out working Lightning, and I haven't any notion where Jewelene is." She laughed lightly, and her eyes took on some animation. "Jewel is forever up to something."

"The wonder is that she should leave my cousin to . . . Miss Clay's devices," mused Keith aloud.

Elizabeth took instant umbrage. She loved Jewelene and was not backward for all her shyness. "I beg your pardon, sir."

Keith was slightly amused. "Do you? I meant only that I had imagined Miss Henshaw would be more interested in entertaining the dowager's son herself, rather than leaving him to another."

She drew her brows together and sighed, "You don't understand. Normally, Jewelene is a perfect hostess. But . . . well, we depend on her so. This estate, though its management goes to Sir James, is largely run by Jewelene. She is the elder, you see, and she is determined that Jimmy shall continue at the university."

At that moment the parlor door opened wide to admit Jewelene. The marquess turned his attention from Elizabeth and caught his breath in spite of himself. Jewelene was a beautiful sight to see—rosy cheeks, sparkling green eyes, and a smile as sweet as spring.

"Hello. How have you all been going on?"

Before anyone could respond, the door behind her opened once again, and Sir James and Ben Clay entered.

Jewelene spun round and went toward them, her hand outstretched.

Ben Clay put it up to his lips, and his eyes twinkled as he said, "Miss Henshaw," there was the familiar tease in his voice, "I am delighted to see you looking so well."

"And I you, sir," she responded at once, then turned to her brother. "Jimmy . . . come, I want to speak to you about Lightning," with which she took him aside.

Keith had not missed the look that passed between Jewelene and Ben Clay. He had sat oddly rigid while he watched, aware of a strange sensation throughout his body. However, he could find no logical reason for it, try as he might.

Elizabeth watched Ben Clay and her cousin and felt a miserable constriction in her throat which was not so easily dismissed, for she knew well the cause. She had been far too attracted to the large, quiet Ben Clay from the first time they had met some months ago. They had not seen each other often, but she knew her heart. Herein lay the problem. Ben Clay's attention seemed centered on Jewelene, and now it would appear that Jewelene was beginning to reciprocate that admiration. It had not always been so, thought Elizabeth now, but there was no denying that something was going on between the pair. And being who she was, she told herself she must wish her cousin happiness and forget her own feelings for Ben Clay.

Lyla saw what passed between her brother and Jewelene, and her eyes narrowed. However, at the moment she could not be bothered, for she was busy enchanting the plump marquess at her side. She gave a little crow of delight at seeing Sir James and went toward him, hoping fervently that she was making the marquess livid with jealousy. Had she been more observant, she would have realized that the sudden shifting of Robby in his chair denoted a certain relief.

The parlor doors opened once again, and this time the butler announced luncheon. Jewelene took command, dropping off her conversation with Sir James to set things in order. She had been watching from the corner of her eye and had fully noted the fact that Elizabeth sat somewhat rigidly beside Keith who seemed to be attempting a flirtation with her. For a moment Jewel felt a tightening of her nerves. What if gentle Elizabeth were to come under that rakehell's charms? Then she saw Ben. He had been standing a bit aside conversing with Robby, but his eyes strayed now and then to the couple in the corner of the room. Suddenly, he found the opportunity to put a question to Keith which brought him to their company, and he was bending low over Elizabeth's hand.

Jewelene rushed to them, motioning to Lyla and Sir James as she moved. "Jimmy, you take Lyla in . . ." She looked up to find her aunt entering the room and breathed a sigh of relief. Just in time, she thought. "My lord," she motioned to Robby, ". . . my aunt . . ."

"But, of course," said Robby rising swiftly to the occasion, pleased to be freed from Lyla Clay.

"Ben . . . Elizabeth. Mr. Robendale and I will bring up the rear," she smiled sweetly. "Shall we go in?"

Ten

The sun peeped between fingers of gilt-edged cloud, and the sky turned bright azure. A breeze stirred the flounce of Jewelene's spencer and played with Sir James's open buckskin riding coat. His uncovered brown hair curled about his fair face, and he smiled broadly.

"Put him through his paces and, I tell you, girl, he did splendidly. Lord, but he'll do."

Jewelene smiled. She had wanted to go walking on her own and was but giving him half her attention. Normally she welcomed his company, for she had not hitherto enjoyed solitude, but for some unknown reason she had suddenly needed to go down to the seaside and think.

"I am well aware of Lightning's prowess, my pup. You are telling me nothing new."

"Yes, but I wished to set your mind at ease. Methinks, girl, you are fretting and fratching about the entrance fee. Don't have to anymore. Arthur and I have thought of a solution."

She turned to look at him, somewhat taken aback and just a bit wary. "Have you? What, then? Give over, do!"

"Can't. And that end of it doesn't matter now, does it, so long as we get the thing done. Which is why I wanted to speak to you alone." He took a breath, "I'm off tomorrow morning for the mainland."

"What?" she ejaculated, much surprised. "But, Jimmy, you can't . . . not now with our house guests upon us."

"Can—and what's more—must! Don't want you to worry about it, but there it is. Must go, and don't ask me for details. Can't speak about such things to a woman," he added mysteriously.

"What the deuce? Jimmy . . ." she threatened.

He ignored her tone. "Won't be gone above a week and, when we return, we'll be set right and tight, see if we won't."

"But, Jimmy, it isn't necessary," she put in quickly. "Ben . . . Ben has this plan and . . ."

"And I'm not leaving Henshaw problems to Ben Clay. Lord, girl, I'm a man full grown for all you treat me like a moonling! 'Tis my problem to deal with, and so I shall."

She laughed in spite of herself, proud of his backbone. "Very well, then. Not a moonling but still somewhat green, and greener still if you won't admit to it!"

He smiled ruefully. "You may be out there. Downy as you are, Jewelene, you are just a woman . . . and some things are best left to a man!" He moved away from her. "There now, I've a host of things to do . . ."

"Jimmy! This discussion has not ended!" she warned.

"Now don't be flying into the boughs, m'girl. What, did you think I had no more pluck than a dunghill cock? Did you? Well, it won't serve! I am every bit a Henshaw and mean to have at this problem. We need the entrance fee and, by God, I am going to see that we get it!"

"Yes, but how?" she begged.

"Arthur knows someone . . . if you must know. It is . . . something in the nature of a loan . . ."

"Oh, no, Jimmy . . ."

"Buck up, old girl." Then moving firmly away, "I'm off, so let's have no more talk of it. I leave in the morning, and that is final."

She watched him stalk off and sighed. He was right. He was a Henshaw which meant he had a stubborn streak.

Well, there was nothing for it. If he was set on taking out a personal loan, they would repay it with what she made at the Silver Heart for she was not about to have any more debts hanging over her head.

She turned and made for the west field and the sea, but a call brought her head round. Odd, she thought, how his voice had the power to make her jump. She waited as Keith, his ginger tresses blowing about his handsome face, made his way toward her.

She had left him in the library, pleased to see that he no longer occupied a seat beside her cousin, still more pleased to feel his eyes follow her out of the room. Rakehell, libertine, she thought, after Babette one moment and me the next. This, though absurd as it was, amused her and she smiled in spite of herself.

He saw the laughter in her green eyes, and the sparkle sent a thrill through him. Something had been troubling him since luncheon. It had kept him quiet, thoughtful, observant, but he could not bring it to a head. He simply could not determine what was nagging at the back of his mind.

"Miss Henshaw . . . I noticed you out walking and, as the others have got up a game of whist, I thought I might join you."

She had wanted to be alone, but it appeared that this was not something she was going to attain. She gave up. "Of course, Mr. Robendale," she said amiably.

"Do you think you might find it in your heart to call me Keith? It would be so much more comfortable," he suggested easily.

She smiled. She liked informalities and saw nothing improper in it. After all, he was a houseguest. "I should be delighted, sir."

"And may I call you Jewelene?" he pursued.

She inclined her head but quickly changed the subject, for she could feel a hot flush steal to her cheeks. Ridiculous, she thought. Why the deuce did he always put her to the blush over nothing?

Naughtily she said, "Did you ever find your way to the Silver Heart?"

His brow went up. "Indeed. Your brother was quite right. Ben Clay runs an exceptional establishment."

"Ah! The stakes then were to your liking? Did you play at E.O.?" She didn't know why she was doing this.

"E.O.? How would you know about such things?" he teased.

"Oh, you must know my father was quite a gamester himself. It was papa who set Ben up in business after Ben returned from the War . . ." she said reminiscently.

"Ah, I see." he said, frowning.

She looked at him. "No, you don't. You are thinking what an odd thing to do, to set up a young gentleman in an ungenteel establishment. But you don't know. When Ben returned . . . maimed . . . depressed, and found his mother much in debt with no way out . . . well, the Silver Heart was a godsend . . . and something he turned to quite good account."

"You and he . . . are very close?" he asked feeling a strange tenseness.

"Oh, yes," she answered simply.

This reply did nothing to satisfy a question that had been quietly plaguing his mind. He pursued. "The wonder is that you and he . . . well . . . one might suppose . . . ?"

She glanced at him sidewise, caught his meaning, and gave a titter.

"Do you find that such a wonder?" she asked.

"Yes, yes, I do. But then perhaps I speak out of turn. It may be that Mr. Clay's interests lie elsewhere," he suggested boldly, watching her closely, thinking of Babette. Was there something in the way Jewelene moved her head . . .

"Oh, as to that, Ben is not involved with anyone," she asserted.

"You think not?" Keith sounded somewhat annoyed.

"I know he is not," she said glibly.

"I see."

"But we have deviated, sir," she put in, abruptly changing the subject. "It was about your evening that we were speaking. Did you play at E.O.?"

"As a matter of fact, the spin of a ball has never really intrigued me. I am a gamester, yes, but I like some of the odds in my favor!"

"Then what did you play at?" she asked, repressing all her conscious better sense.

"I put a hand in at the faro table," he said shortly, evidently not wishing to discuss it.

"Oh? And did you win?" she asked sweetly.

He gazed at her a moment before smiling. "No, as a matter of fact, I lost a great deal more than I intended. But, no matter, I shall see it righted tonight."

"Oh, then you consider yourself a master at faro? I play a little myself, but I always understood from Papa it was a prodigiously difficult thing to handle."

"It is and, though I prefer écarté . . . I have considered myself not quite a commoner at faro. I am, after all . . . a gamester by need," he reminded her gently, lest she be forgetting.

She felt very much like retorting that Babette had deemed otherwise, so loose had he been with his wagers, however, she controlled her tongue and said instead, "Oh, yes, you had said your only means of survival is the gaming tables." She sighed mockingly. "A sorry lot to be a second son. Well, never mind, perhaps tonight you will recoup your losses. Indeed, sir," she added mischievously, "I wish you luck."

He looked at her. There was something about the quality of her voice, the tease that carried to her eyes, that took him aback. Everything about her seemed to tantalize him. An odd thing that, he thought to himself, that he could be so equally attracted to two women so totally different and desire both at the same time.

Many hours later, the Marquess of Lyndhurst sat beside Babette at the faro table and again wondered about that very same thing. Babette sparkled in a simple but most alluring gown of silver sarcenet and satin. Her black hair tickled her face whenever she moved. A long, silver-painted feather curled round her tresses and touched her shoulder, and her black mask intrigued all who saw her.

And ah, how Jewelene did deceive. It took all her wits and ingenuity to keep her admirers faithful and pleased to be sporting the blunt, laying it across the table, losing it to the house with grins and puppy-dog eyes. Then there were the more sophisticated blades at her table, eying her curiously, flirting with deeper, grosser intent. She handled them all most deftly, and the marquess could not but admire her style. Indeed, the Frenchwoman had a great deal of style. Filey and Hill were staunch to her reign, and Babette played with them outrageously, secretly pleased to keep them near, somewhat fending off the older, more experienced rakes. However, this night the marquess had positioned himself at her elbow, and he played a far more determined game. He wanted her and every move, every word was calculated to that end.

"La, m'sieur . . ." she was answering his dallying, ". . . you flatter me much . . . I know not how to answer such a pretty remark."

"I can think of a very excellent answer, my beauty. Shall I tell it to you?" he returned softly, his eyes locking with hers. She stirred him, yes, but there was something more, something that kept him nearly mesmerized. It was as though he played with some puzzle and knew some pieces were missing.

Jewelene laughed sweetly, stalling, for she was running out of answers. And then she felt as though her heart had lost the ability to function. Lord Omsbury had walked into the room. He stood there like some magnetic demon. The candlelight from the wall sconces and the chandelier above his head seemed to pick up the silver tints in his dark hair and glint them wickedly into Jewelene's eyes. He scrutinized the entire room, pausing as his eyes found her. He scanned her from head to toe, one mobile brow going up before he dismissed her from his thoughts. Another time perhaps he may have been enticed but not now. No, not when his every thought held visions of Jewelene Henshaw's honey tresses and green eyes. Not when his every need called for that elusive vision. He was obsessed by the fantasy of possessing her. Never before had he wanted a woman to wife—perhaps he did not now—but she was quality. There was no other way of obtaining her.

Jewelene's thoughts brought her near to panic. She saw the demon before her, and her knees grew weak. If he were to discover her disguise, she would be undone. He could then force her to marriage with the threat of ruining her name and bringing shame to her brother, her aunt, and

Elizabeth. Oh, God! She was suddenly struck with the enormity of her crime. Then he turned his back and moved toward Ben and the E.O. table. She saw Ben standing taut and still, watching her, and a look passed between them before she breathed again in relief.

Her table noticed only that she had taken overlong in the deal; however, the Marquess of Lyndhurst noticed much, much more, and he frowned. He had seen the effect Omsbury's entrance had had upon her, he had seen the relief when Omsbury moved away, and he had seen also the look that had crossed the room between Ben Clay and Babette. He was nettled by it. What in thunder did it all mean? He had to know, *he would* know, and he would *not* give up until all these questions were satisfactorily answered.

Omsbury noticed nothing except that Ben Clay seemed rather nervous; a state he had not hitherto noticed in the one-armed gentleman. He smiled smugly, certain that this was due to the notes he held over the fellow's head. He placed his bet on number twenty, stacking his rouleaux neatly on the board and saying without meeting Ben's eyes,

"A new faro dealer, I see."

Ben called in all bets before glancing sidewise at him.

"Babette? Yes, and quite an addition to my modest establishment. Quite lovely and an excellent dealer as well. You, I am persuaded, my lord, will not find her an easy adversary," said Ben carefully.

"No? But then I have no notion of taking her on. Faro and I have never gone on well together. I rather fancy at this stage of my life to take on a completely new role and with a beauty of a far different stamp from that raven-haired creature you have there."

Ben dropped the little white ball into the spin of the wheel, and both men watched as it took its time, clanking saucily, teasing the eyes of those who had placed bets on its fall.

"I have no notion to what you allude," said Ben cautiously. The ball landed on number seven. He called it out and motioned Silas to collect for the house, looking meaningfully at Omsbury as Silas's hooked stick made them aware of his lordship's loss.

Omsbury frowned. "I may lose at your tables, sir, but not, I assure you, at anything else I tackle."

Ben's smile held no warmth. "Your bet, my lord?"

"Clay, may I remind you . . . just what I hold over your head. It will be to your interest to aid me in my endeavors!" hissed Omsbury.

"Are you suggesting, my lord, that I advise you how to go on?" asked Ben sardonically. "Why . . . I would have to be daft to bet against my own house, and mark me, sir, that is exactly what such a move would be, bringing down m'own house!"

Omsbury did not lose Ben's meaning. He knew full well that while no romantic attachment existed between Jewelene Henshaw and Ben Clay, they were unaccountably close. They seemed to feel they owed one another an uncommon loyalty. This he meant to use to his advantage for he knew that Jewelene would not stand by and allow Ben Clay to be destroyed. He had, in addition to the five-thousand-pound note, discovered that Clay's establishment was covered by a twenty-thousand-pound mortgage and one that he could—for a price—purchase. He thought of Jewelene at that moment, and the price did not seem too steep. He smiled wickedly.

"No, sir, you would not do so willingly, but I am not set

back by such as that." He laid another heavy bet on the board. "You see, Clay, I continue the game."

Jewelene at her table played a bad hand, taking a slight loss for the house. She had been inattentive, her eyes darting across the room to Ben and Omsbury and then sustaining yet another shock. Her hand fluttered on its path to her forehead, and her cheeks went white. She had heard his voice even before he came upon the scene, but she was unwilling to believe her ears. It couldn't be . . . he didn't even like gambling . . . but it was—Jimmy! She watched, horrified, as Sir James, arm in arm with his crony, Arthur Salford, walked in upon them.

Eleven

Jewelene blanched, and one hand gripped the table edge for support. She would never be able to deceive Jimmy. There was not a chance of it, and she surely would have them all burnt if she tried; likely as not, he'd give her away from pure astonishment. She had to escape, there was nothing for it, she had to get away before he spotted her.

"Babette . . . little love . . ." said the marquess, coming to her aid, his hand steadying her elbow. He had noticed her sudden loss of color. "Whatever is wrong? Are you ill?"

"I . . . oh, *oui*, monsieur . . . I feel overly warm . . . faint . . ." she turned her back toward her brother and called to her lookout boy, "Jem . . . eh . . . you will take zee table for me . . ."

"Allow me to escort you," cried Filey, jumping to his feet.

"No, me!" shouted Hill, not to be outdone.

The marquess said nothing as he glanced imperiously down at them and led the lady away. "So kind of you, m'sieur . . ." she said softly, thankful for his wide shoulders, leaning heavily into him to conceal herself from her brother. She could just see from beneath her lashes that Jimmy and Arthur had moved to the black ombre table. The marquess's observant eye followed her glance, and his brow went up. What had *she* to do with Sir James? They had just about reached the exit when Jimmy's voice bellowed out. "So, there you are, Mr. Robendale! Your cousin pointed us in this direction. Said you were determined to recoup your losses of the other night, but I did not at first perceive . . ."

"Sir James . . . I shall be back in a moment . . ." said his lordship, hastening to keep up with the lady fleeing before him.

Much surprised but not at all perturbed, Jimmy said to the marquess's retreating form, "Oh . . . yes . . . quite . . ." and turned to his friend.

The marquess caught up with Babette, took her arm once again, and found that she was leading him down the hall to a gilt-moulded door. This opened into Ben's chamber. She turned at the portal and attempted a dismissal. "*Merci, m'sieur,* you were so good . . . now I think . . . I shall just lie down for a spell . . ."

He moved in adroitly, gently tooling her towards the sofa. "Ah, but what sort of knave do you take me for? Leave a damsel in distress?" ignoring her protests, "Lie back, Babette, and close your eyes . . . I'll just pour you a glass of brandy."

She did as he suggested, feeling he might go away once he saw her comfortable. She opened her eyes to find him sitting over her. She raised herself on her elbows. "There's the good girl . . ." he said, putting the brandy to her lips. Their eyes met and she felt suddenly a strange, almost suffocating sensation. He put the glass down, his eyes still holding her, and his arm slid round her back, drawing her to him. She knew what he was about to do and knew she should be stopping him but could not. His mouth closed on hers, at first gently, tenderly, and then his arms tightened.

The door at his back opened, and a shocked harsh voice snapped, "Mr. Robendale!"

Jewelene pulled out of the marquess's hold and gasped to see Ben furious above them. The marquess jumped to his feet but said nothing for a moment and, when he did, it was with full composure, "Ah, Mr. Clay, it is *your* office I know . . . but it would seem your presence at the moment is quite . . . *de trop* . . ." It was amiably said, and Ben could see the amusement in Keith's gray eyes.

"Is it?" he returned glancing towards Jewelene, the question on his face. She shook her head gently as though to tell him to be calm. He understood but took a stand, "It may interest you to know, Mr. Robendale, that *Babette is spoken for*." There, he had done it, taken her out of reach. And really what harm could it do him? None, and it was the answer for it would serve to spare her further such encounters.

"Oh?" said the marquess, his brow going up, his temper suddenly kindled. There was something wrong here, something smoky, and he had no liking for feeling the fool. "The lady gave me no indication . . ."

"No, sir," she interrupted him at once. "There was so little opportunity . . . and it . . . is not altogether the case . . . is it, *chéri?*" looking toward Ben.

"Is it not, Babette?" admonished Ben, doing it rather brown. "You wound me, love."

She looked daggers at him. It was preposterous, she knew, but she did not want Keith walking away thinking so very wickedly of her. After all. . . she had just allowed him to kiss her, and now Ben would have him think her a betrothed lady. She blushed, "Well, what I mean is . . . ah . . . zees eez zo complicated . . ." she stalled for words and looked to Ben for help. He had an irresistible urge to chuckle at her dilemma but controlled himself.

The marquess was far too observant for such a frivolous pair. Again his brows went up, but he listened quietly to Babette as she concluded the dialogue.

"Ours . . . has always been . . . such . . . a . . . friendly . . . arrangement . . ." Again she glanced toward Ben and the tips of her curved mouth began to quiver, ". . . that I nearly always forget that . . . we have recently decided to make it . . . a lasting one."

The marquess eyed her dubiously. Damn! Who was this brazen little beauty? He wished very much that Ben Clay had not entered at that inopportune time for a moment more would have seen Babette's mask removed.

"Indeed, Mr. Clay . . . it would appear that I must needs offer my apologies . . . and congratulations in one!" He turned and bowed towards Babette but his eyes were hard as steel. "However, I shall still look forward to mamselle's speedy recovery and her return to the faro table as soon as may be." With that he turned and left them.

Jewelene dared not glance at Ben for some time afterward and, when she finally looked his way, she was thrown into convulsive laughter.

He chuckled with her but admonished at length. "My dear little hoyden, do you realize that your brother is out there listening to tales of the beautiful masked French vixen and demanding to meet her!"

"Oh, no!" she cried in dismay. "Tell him to be off . . . anything . . . only get him to leave." He gazed for a long time at her. "Jewelene . . . may I suggest at this point that the game outwits us?"

"You may. However, may I suggest that it is extremely poor-spirited of you to suggest it?" she bantered.

"You are a ramshackle, tumbledown chit!"

"And a sore trial to boot. Do go and put my brother off, Ben. And then later, we must talk, but not now. We can't both be absent from the tables. The men might start to talk."

He sighed. "Very well, brat. I shall endeavor to do your bidding, though every good sense I have tells me 'tis time to send you packing!"

She watched him go, beaming wide until the door had closed at his back. The smile suddenly disappeared. She was beginning to wonder if he was right. But they needed the entrance fee to get Lightning into the race, and she just couldn't give up now. And then something else tugged at her mind and heart. It was, of course, that dratted gamester . . . that rakehell fiend . . . that charmer, Keith Robendale. He had kissed her and made her feel . . . she wasn't quite sure what. A perfectly terrible man he was, to be sure. He had flirted and laughed with Jewelene today as though she were the only woman in the world and now. . . now here he was, seducing Babette!

"Jimmy! Where have you been, you young pup?" cried Filey, jumping to his feet and slapping Sir James soundly on the back. They were some years apart, Filey being the elder, but they had on several occasions enjoyed one another's company at a local spot or two. "And Art, old boy . . . good to see you. But this isn't one of your haunts. What's to do?"

Sir James smiled good-naturedly. "Art and I are off in the morning for the mainland, and he had this 'feeling' that he might win against that nasty little ball over there . . ." nodding toward the E.O. table, "thereby adding to his already plump pockets."

"Well, then, go to it my friend, and better stick to that table, for you don't stand a chance at faro."

"No, that I don't," agreed Arthur. He was a tall, lean lad with a shock of unruly hair and uncoordinated clothing, but he came from good stock, and his disposition made him in general a favorite among the local *ton*.

"Ay. But you said it strangely, Filey. What's toward?" asked Sir James looking in the direction of the young boy dealing at the faro table.

"Oh, not him," said Filey contemptuously. "He deals well enough . . . but there ain't nothing to match Babette!"

"Babette? Who the deuce is she?" inquired Jimmy.

"A beauty of a French chit . . ." sighed Filey, "with raven locks and green eyes . . . at least, I think they're green . . . can't really tell with that devilish mask she wears. . . ."

"Mask?" ejaculated Jimmy, "Lord, but that's good. What in thunder has Ben been at? Employing wenches with masks? Damned improper, I say," he said, laughing.

"Indeed. Has each and every one of us trying to discover who she really is," said Filey. "Good sport . . . in fact, Hill here started a betting book on it. We've all had a guess and logged it."

Sir James grinned. "If that don't beat all! Damned bunch of twiddle-poops you are—each and every one bothering your heads about such things!" He looked up and spotted the marquess entering the room. "Arthur, come along. Want you to meet m'houseguest. Nice chap. You'll like him."

The marquess looked up to see Sir James bowling down upon him. He liked James Henshaw, he was a nice plucky lad. He wondered what it was that had brought him to the Silver Heart . . . surely the Henshaws were in no position to be gambling what little blunt they had?

"Sir James, so sorry I had to run out on you earlier," apologized the marquess quietly.

"Well, as to that . . . don't mean to sit in your pocket, Mr. Robendale. Should have realized you were . . . engaged . . ." said Sir James, tactfully avoiding questioning him about the woman he had scarcely noticed. He then proceeded to make known to him the lanky fellow fidgeting at his side. Keith smiled and acknowledged the young man before dropping his voice and saying softly, "What . . . er . . . brings you here, Jimmy, my boy?"

"Art here had a notion to place a bet or two . . . but in truth, we met your cousin at the White Stag down the street, and he said you would probably be here. Thought I'd drop by and take my leave of you as we will be off too early tomorrow morning to do the thing then."

"Off tomorrow?" frowned the marquis, "You are leaving the isle?"

"Ay. Going to the mainland. Portsmouth . . ." put in Arthur, then dropping his voice portentously, "Have some business of sorts to conclude . . . Lightning 'n' all . . . rather private matter, sticky too . . . nothing havey-cavey, mind, but . . ."

"Mummer it, Art!" snapped Sir James eying his friend repressingly. He smiled apologetically at the marquess. "Good fellow, Arthur . . . but a sad rattle." Again he eyed his friend, daring him to challenge this pronouncement. Arthur smiled rather blankly, and Sir James shook his head. "Well, that's it then. Couldn't leave without . . . well, *there* you are, Ben!"

Ben Clay grinned, but his voice when he spoke held a note of disapproval. "Jimmy. Good to see you, though I ain't pleased to see you *here*."

"Eh? Oh, worried about m'losing m'ready to your house?" laughed Sir James, not at all affronted. "Don't fratch over it, Ben. Have no mind or hand for chancy ways! And besides wouldn't be putting *you* into a rare kick-up . . . Jewelene would have m'head!"

"And mine!" agreed Ben, laughing. "Then what are you doing here? And don't be putting the blame on poor Arthur." He reached out and patted Arthur's shoulder, "How are you, old boy?"

Arthur advised him that he was pretty stout, and Ben turned again to Sir James. "Well then, Jimmy, as I was saying, what are you doing here?"

"Just came to bid Keith here fare thee well, so don't be looking down so at me," rallied Sir James. "Jewel bade me earlier to do the thing. Houseguest and all . . . said it wasn't the thing leaving her to . . . well . . ." seeing that he was nearly about to commit a social blunder, he blushed and said instead, "Well, forgot to do it earlier . . ."

"Oh? You off somewhere?" asked Ben, frowning.

"Ay, Portsmouth," stated Arthur, pleased to be able to say something and quite ready to give over to his loquacious nature.

"Never mind," put in Jimmy hastily. "We don't need you to be chucking at us again."

"Why though, Jimmy?" pursued Ben.

Jimmy glanced at Keith and blushed again. "Don't worry, Ben, I don't mean to get burnt in one week. Trust

Jewelene to hold household while I'm gone . . . and speaking of going, we had better be off, Art." He waved to them as he started for the door. "Catching the yawl to Portsmouth at eight . . . see you in a week's time!"

Ben and the Marquess of Lyndhurst stood quietly, both frowning, both wondering as they wished Sir James and his friend a good trip. And then the lads were gone, leaving the older men to their conjectures. During his stay at the Silver Heart, Sir James had never once noticed Lord Omsbury at the E.O. table, never once noticed Omsbury hovering about in the background. But he had been there . . . though somewhat out of view!

Omsbury had been all too interested to learn that Sir James was leaving for Portsmouth. He was all too engrossed with Art's disjointed eloquence regarding Lightning . . . what had the boys to do in Portsmouth regarding that horse? He had no wish for Lightning to make it to Derby. He knew what that stallion was capable of and couldn't take the chance of allowing the Henshaws a win at Derby. So . . . Sir James was taking the yawl at eight?

The marquess saw a movement just behind the straw-colored velvet drapes. His observant eyes followed the line down to the oriental carpet and saw there bright shining hessians. He waited and had not a long period to discover the owner of these boots to be Lord Omsbury. Devil a bit! Why would Omsbury be spying on Sir James? What could possibly interest such a man about the movements of a stripling? To be sure, Omsbury was after the stripling's sister but . . . and yet, the marquess rather fancied he was beginning to understand.

He would have to think on this later, now he had something else, something far more pressing on his mind. "Clay?" he called.

Ben turned half way, "Yes, Mr. Robendale?"

"Shall we not find how our lady does?"

"I was just about to send a lackey to ask after her needs," said he, forgetting to be the possessive lover. The marquess could not help but notice this. Now had the lady been his, had Clay been the interloper, he would have been quick to take objection to the *"our lady."* He would have been quick to reiterate the fact that she was his, but Ben Clay had neglected to do this. Odd that!

"Ah . . . yes, and do have him tell her that we *all* await her return most fervently . . . all, that is, except Sir James. A pity the lad won't have the opportunity to meet our pretty Babette." He didn't know why he had said that last. It had come to him suddenly, more as an afterthought, and he was as much startled by Ben Clay's reaction as Ben Clay was by his statement. Eh, he thought, what have I stumbled upon? *Who the devil is this Babette?*

Twelve

It was scarcely one in the morning when Omsbury dismounted in his stables and began shouting for his groom. He was in a black mood, as indeed he had been most of this past month.

"Jenkins . . . Jenkins, you blackguard . . . sleeping are you? Get your butt down here!" He picked up a martingale, fingering its brass while he waited, listening to the shuffling of feet abovestairs. It would seem his groom was not alone. "Fiend seize your soul! Jenkins, how long am I to be kept waiting?"

A wiry little man with small dark eyes and a shock of unruly grayish hair appeared at the top of the stairs. He was putting on a wool knit sweater, holding his short, wool coat with one hand. "Aye, m'lord . . . aye . . ." he said as he took the steps from his room to the floor below.

Omsbury looked past him to the crack at Jenkins's door. The pale light of a nightstand candle glowed, and he saw the ruffle of a skirt as the lady inside looked for a place in which to conceal herself. He smiled ruefully to himself and then looked his groom over. "My, my, Jenkins, you never cease to astonish me with your prowess." Then as though brushing this slight diversion away, his face became grim once more. "I want you on your way to Cowes! Get those lazy seamen of mine up and my sloop out as soon as possible. I want you docked in Portsmouth by dawn and then, Jenkins, I have a special assignment for you."

"Aye, m'lord. Trust me to do as ye wishes," said Jenkins.

"I trust you to do what will get you a pretty fee," said Omsbury with total disdain.

Jenkins said nothing to this, but his eyes were alert as he waited for his lordship to continue.

"Very well, then. We have you at Portsmouth. You will await the docking of the eight o'clock yawl and will watch for one passenger in particular."

"Who might that be, and 'ow will I be knowing him?"

"Oh, you know him. All of Wight knows him. He is Sir James," said Omsbury, a sneer distorting his features.

"Aye," said Jenkins, his eyes opening wider, "Sir James, is it?"

"That's right. Are you quite ready, Jenkins? Do you think I may now proceed?" demanded his lordship sardonically.

"Aye," said Jenkins not at all abashed.

The marquess gave his horse to a link boy and bade him walk the steed outside the doors of the White Stag. He could hear the revelry indoors and through the undraped windows he could see tankards of ale waving to song. His brow went up with amusement. It would appear that his cousin had been enjoying himself.

He walked in and stood at the threshold a moment, getting his bearings and surveying the room for signs of Rob. He spotted him with a group of fashionable young men who were gathered round an enormous and somewhat battered oak table. They seemed deep in amiable though controversial discussion. The marquess drew near, picking up bits and pieces of the argument on his way. It seemed to concern the very exciting match scheduled for the following week and which had brought all these corinthians from the mainland.

"I say Jackson could have whipped them both . . ." put in Robby glaring down a somewhat younger fellow at his elbow. "Never was such a bruiser . . . no other pealed like Jackson, I tell you!"

"Noddy!" uttered a gentleman of some girth and years, coming up behind Robby and causing Rob to turn his head uncomfortably in his collar. "Tosh and nonsense! The Gentleman Jackson pealed to advantage in his day, but his day has been over some years now! Pups, the lot of you . . . why in my day . . ."

"In your day you had the Black and Jackson! *We still* have Jackson, and I tell you he is the best!" put in Rob.

"Verily, verily . . ." tittered a young blood across the table who had imbibed beyond his capacity.

"Yea! I agree with Rob here. Jackson is the best," said another.

"Lobcocks, the whole blasted lot of you! Why, this man Sawyers would put the Gentleman Jackson to the blush . . ." said the older man, his cheeks puffing out.

"Sacrilege!" laughed yet another good fellow.

The marquess tapped his cousin's shoulder. Robby turned round, focused, and then beamed wide. "Keith? You here? Excellent . . . excellent. Tell these fools . . ."

"Not now, coz! We're off . . ." said the marquess quietly, his grin taking in the interested glances cast his way.

"No? Off? Are we . . . why?"

"It is necessary. Believe me. 'Tis time you bid your friends good night and came away with me. You'll thank me in the morning."

"Oh. Very well," said Robby amiably. His nature was the sweetest imaginable whether he was in his cups or no. It came through to his brain that his cousin wished to depart this jolly set. Now, while he would have enjoyed to linger another hour or two, he would on no account disoblige a friend, especially one that was a dear and most beloved cousin as well.

"Up with you, sweetheart," laughed the marquess, helping his inebriated cousin to his feet.

"Good of you, old boy . . ." said Robby.

"What, and are you leaving us?" cried a young man, cutting the discussion short. "Never say so? Who the devil is this fellow taking you off?"

Robby gazed at the man a moment and then began a low chuckle, "Why . . . he is . . . me . . ." at which he gave over to whoops.

"Shhh . . ." whispered the marquess waving himself and his cousin off. "Good night, lads . . . and just to set you all straight. There never was one that could beat Gentleman Jackson, and there still is not! He uses more than his brawn, my bucks . . . keep that in mind." With which he left them staring after his large broad back.

Some time afterward, mounted and on their way to Henshaw House, Robby was still chuckling over his private little jest. The marquess glanced his way and sighed.

"More than half-foxed you are, my boy."

"What . . . me? Never. Fit as a fiddle . . . though I am in m'cups . . . but . . . no more than a trifle . . ." answered Robby.

"That's good. Have something of a problem picking at me. But don't know if you are . . . well enough to lend assistance?" He was grinning again, watching his cousin reposition himself carefully in the saddle, adding, "Easy there, Rob . . . don't be falling off."

"What? Me . . . fall off?" returned the Honorable Oscar Robendale, evidently thinking his cousin had taken leave of his senses.

"So sorry, Rob. How could I think such a thing?" chuckled the marquess.

"Humph," said Robby. "Now . . . what's this problem," he asked. "Go on . . . have at me."

"Oh, no. Not tonight," said Keith, "not in your present condition."

"Present condition? Well! I like that. I mean, Keith, really . . . I know what I'm about. I ain't denying that I feel a trifle lightheaded . . . but . . ."

"Very well . . ." laughed the marquess, "maybe you are right. Perhaps it does need a befuddled brain to work out this muddle."

Two figures left the rear entrance of the home Ben Clay shared with his mother and sister. Jewelene was once again in breeches. A dark cloak hung about her, its front corner panel slung backwards over one shoulder, her hood low over her forehead. Ben's hand rested beneath her elbow as he led her to their waiting horses. He hoisted her into her saddle. She looked about her and said in a low voice,

"You do think we've given Keith Robendale and his cousin time to get to Henshaw House?"

"Yes . . . and it's late, puss . . . come on," he said, nimbly climbing into his own saddle. Then they bounded forward, taking the cobblestone street only as far as the first stye, then into the fields heading toward Jewelene's home.

The early morning mist hung about their horses' fetlocks in mysterious formations, and a breeze brought some mist to Jewelene's cheeks. She loved it and smiled to herself. However, a glance at her friend told her he was troubled. What was wrong? It was not the first time she had seen such a look come over him. He was fratching himself over something, and she was fairly certain it had naught to do with her. She brought in rein, slowing her horse and he followed suit, glancing her way.

"What's toward, Ben? You are looking as down as a muckworm."

"Good Lord, Jewel . . . a muckworm is it? Could you not search your vocabulary for a better comparison?" But he was smiling.

"Seriously, Ben. Something is wrong. What is it?"

"Naught. Now for once be a good little girl, and don't plague me."

"Little girl, eh?" she took amiable exception. She remembered something that had intrigued her that afternoon. She had seen the way Ben's eyes had lingered on her cousin, Liz. In fact, she had been much surprised by it. She meant only to tease him now. She certainly had no way of knowing the reaction she was about to get. "Why, fancy your thinking so when I am at least a year older than my cousin, Elizabeth . . . and, la, Ben, if I didn't see you looking at her in *such* a way. One would never suppose you thought *her* a little girl, for you looked much like a naughty spider in hopes of . . ."

He cut her off harshly. "Jewelene!" He was furious. Her eyes opened wide in surprise, but he continued, "That is quite enough!"

She was taken aback. Her small jaw dropped. She felt

no affront, she felt no pique, she felt only pure astonishment and sudden dawning.

What then? Ben and Elizabeth? Of course! How could she have been so blind not to notice . . . not to realize? All those blushes she had seen on Elizabeth whenever Ben came on the scene. His very quiet, odd behavior whenever his eyes gazed upon her . . . Ben and Elizabeth! It was wonderful! Faith, they were perfect for one another . . . it was so right. *And then she remembered her Aunt Dora!*

"Oh goodness!" she said aloud but to herself. However, Ben had not heard. He was too far ahead. "Aunt Dora." Now here was a problem. Aunt Dora was the best of mothers. She was kindhearted and warm and full of schemes for the betterment of her only daughter. She would never countenance an alliance between Ben and Elizabeth . . . not while Ben ran a gambling den.

Ben slowed his horse. He had been too rough on Jewel. She had only meant to jest. It was true . . . he did always think of her as younger than Elizabeth. It was, he supposed, because of Elizabeth's womanly air. She had such grace . . . such beauty . . . such wisdom. He ached at the thought of her. He sent a glance over his shoulder and saw the set of Jewelene's shoulders. Oh, poor chit, she was looking down. He felt a stab of guilt and slowed his horse.

Jewelene was, in fact, troubled by this new revelation. She would have to come up with some notion or other to arrange things for poor Ben and Elizabeth. So when she found him abreast she did not immediately smile.

He sighed, "Look, puss . . . don't fret. I'm just foul-tempered at this hour . . ."

"What?" she said coming out of her thoughts. "Oh, foul-tempered, are you? And with good reason, my dear Ben. But never fear, all will be right and tight. Just leave it to me."

His brows went up, and he felt a sudden surge of trepidation. What had entered her head now? "Jewelene?" he said hesitatingly.

She cut him off. "Oh, there, I can just make out the stables. Good night, Ben."

"But?"

She was already riding off. He watched her, his brows drawn, and then he thought of Elizabeth again and sighed before turning his horse back towards Yarmouth.

Omsbury tossed in his bed. Finally he gave up and rose, glancing at his mantelpiece clock. It was past three. Gad, but sleep was a stranger to him these days. It was his obsession driving him mad. His need for two things: to see himself wed to that spitfire Jewelene Henshaw and to ruin Ben Clay. This latter simply because the man had chosen to defy him. Who the devil did he think he was? A skirter to say him, Lord Omsbury, nay? Well, in the end he'd make him crawl! And that stripling, Sir James . . . he'd soon learn what the boy was up to, and it would tighten matters indeed.

He returned to his bed and this time when he laid his head on his down pillow, he was able to close his eyes and put away his plans, secure in their greatness and their inevitable conclusion.

Thirteen

Robby sat over his tomato juice and groaned. One trembling hand swept his light brown hair away from his eyes. He was not feeling quite so fit as he had the previous night. However, he had one thing to be thankful for, and that was the fact that Lyla Clay was not present.

Aunt Dora had scooped that lively schoolgirl out of his way, saying they were off to Yarmouth to visit with Mrs. Clay, and Robby had eyed Aunt Dora much as a puppy dog does some welcome treat. He cared not that Aunt Dora's reasons might be purely selfish, for that lady was determined to get Lyla out of his way only to make a path for either her daughter or her niece.

And so he sat in blissful misery, eyeing his tomato juice and groaning. Jewelene had put her head in at the door to find Robby alone in the breakfast room. This so perfectly suited her mood that she entered, surveyed him with a knowing eye, and told him she had just the cure.

"My mother often prepared the thing for papa . . . and I know that my brother has once or twice had it with perfectly good results."

"Ooo—ooo," said Robby.

She laughed out loud, saw him wince and clapped her hand over her mouth. "Sorry," she whispered and proceeded to fetch him the ingredients she had mentioned. "There," she said, placing the hock and soda water beside the tomato juice. "Now drink it all up and I promise you, you will be the better for it."

He glanced dubiously at the full glasses before him, for

he doubted his ability to hold anything at the moment. But he was too polite to refuse her after she had gone to such trouble. He groaned and began downing the liquids before him.

Much satisfied she turned to go when the gurgling sounds at her back made her realize her brew had already taken effect. With much foresight, she reached for a large Sèvres bowl and shoved it beneath poor Robby's chin whereupon, though much embarrassed, he proceeded to relieve himself.

"That's a dandy!" she said bracingly, "works each and every time. You'll be the better for it." With which she went to the bellpull and summoned a lackey.

"Have the marquess shown to his room when he is feeling more the thing."

Robby glanced up to find her bouncing out of the room, a motion that returned his head to the Sèvres bowl. "Exceptional girl," he thought at his sickest moment.

Jewelene wriggled into her bright blue spencer as she crossed the wide hall to the front doors. Caesar got hastily to his feet, and his black and white tail began to wag. "Oh, want a bit of a run, do you?" she asked him, to which he responded with several affirmative wags. She laughed and opened the door, allowing him to bound outside.

Jewelene smiled at the dog's exuberance. She rather envied him this morning. The late nights were beginning to take their toll on her energy, for she had not even allowed herself to make up for it by sleeping late. Early that morning Jimmy had taken it into his head to pop into her room and shake her merrily but quite rudely, considering the hour wanted nine minutes to seven.

"Wake up, girl . . . I'm off!" he said at his brightest.

"Oh, God!" she said, feeling much in pain.

"No, don't take it like that," he soothed. "I'll be back before you even know I'm gone. Daresay you'll be glad to be rid of me for a few days."

"Oh, God!" was all she could manage. Every inch of her body ached, and she was quite sure she had only minutes ago gotten into bed.

"Well," he said dropping a kiss upon her cheek, "take care, Jewel . . . and don't let that Omsbury knave come calling while I'm gone."

She blinked as the door closed behind him. "O-oh," was all she said before she fell into a fitful sleep. This did not long last for the hour had scarcely reached nine when she had yet another visitor. This time it was her aunt, filled with the happy notion of taking Lyla to visit her mother and hoping the dreadful girl would feel it her duty to remain at home.

"No, auntie, I would like her to return . . . please . . ." said Jewelene, starting to prop herself up. She needed Lyla out of the Clay house. How else could she come and go at such late hours. She could not be seen going into the casino unless she was already disguised, and there was nowhere else to don her costume.

Her aunt sighed as she rose, feeling it wiser to keep silent on the matter, hoping Mrs. Clay would demand her daughter's return, and thus settle the thing for her. However she paused at the door and frowned. "Why . . . Jewelene . . . are you all right?"

"Yes, yes, of course . . ."

"But then . . . 'tis nearly nine . . . what a slug-a-bed you are this morning. Do get up. There is a lovely sun out . . . and you do look a bit pale this morning. Up with you!"

Jewelene sank back onto her pillow when the door

closed, but try as she might she could not get back to sleep. There was nothing for it but to rise, wash, and don a pretty blue muslin gown her maid had laid out for her

What she needed, she told herself now, was a brisk long walk, and the fresh air to dissolve all her fog. And she was riddled with fog. It hung about her eyes, clouding all before her. She had so much to resolve, and nothing seemed to be working out quite as she had planned.

She didn't mind her direction, it didn't really matter, for she was on Henshaw land and therefore free to move at will. She did not notice how close she came to the road. She saw the budding trees and the richness of the evergreens. The land sloped before her, crocus and daffodils swayed in the breeze, and she tried to put everything, all her problems aside, just long enough to enjoy the loveliness of nature in springtime.

But thoughts plow their way against the will. Her problems were numerous, because she cared about others more than she cared about herself.

She had been doing well for the Silver Heart at the faro table, but a dealer's take was not a large one. She doubted very much that she would earn the entrance fee in time. It would appear that she would have to sell her mother's jewels. La, but she did not want to. She was a sentimentalist, a romantic, and those jewels had gone from mother to daughter for generations. Surely, the women of the family had been faced with tight households before. They hadn't sold . . . and it shamed her to think she was forced to it. And then she was rudely, abruptly brought to a sense of her surroundings. For she had nearly walked straight into Omsbury's arms.

"My, my lord . . ." she stammered as she gazed up into his glinting eyes.

"Miss Henshaw," he said bowing. "I saw you from the roadway, hastened to tether my horse, and reach you, that I may accompany your meanderings."

"Really?" she said with some hauteur.

"Ah, you mean to bicker with me already, when I do assure you all I want is to pass a pleasant moment or two. I had thought we might hit a more amiable line of conversation this morning."

"Did you? I can't imagine why."

"May I remind you that within two weeks I shall have your answer regarding our marriage. Why then are you determined to be forever at odds with me?"

"I had not thought you so dense-witted, my lord," she said coldly. "Can you not see that had I any other choice you would have had your answer in the negative immediately? Circumstances have forced me to take your offer into consideration. Only circumstances, for I must . . . indeed, 'tis my duty to advise you beforehand that I cannot like your stamp!"

He glanced at her a long moment, and his eyes were hard, angry, and very determined. "You know, my love, you don't really mean that."

"Don't I? What makes you think so, my lord?" she answered much taken aback.

"Because we are much the same, you and I. Have you not noticed, Jewelene? Allow me then to establish it in your mind. Your beauty, my dear, is of no delicate hue. You need no coddling, no soft words, no petting. Yours is that of a vibrant mare, graceful, wilful, proud! I couldn't bear to have some fairylike creature for wife, forever yeaing me into boredom and, no, you couldn't bear to have some popinjay lord for husband, forever cooing to your whims! You seek just such a man as I.

Jewelene . . . I would wield your fire . . . not burn it out. You were made for the type of life *only I* can give you!"

She gazed at him, her dark brows drawing together for a moment. She was not an unreasonable maid, and there was some truth in what he said. Yes, she didn't want the sort of husband who would coddle her, coo sweetly to her, give her her head in everything. She needed curbing, none knew it better than she, but it would take a very special man to hold her reins. A very special man, not a boy . . . and *not* Omsbury. He was too selfish to ever see outside himself, and there was a streak of meanness in him, a cruelty that lighted his eyes and told her he was past changing. She could never love him. "You are wrong, my lord," she answered quietly. "Oh, indeed . . . I would be lying if I said I didn't need a strong-willed man, a fighter of sorts . . . but he must also be gentle and kind. . . ."

"Like that one-armed skirter, Ben Clay?" he interrupted her harshly, his sneer clear, contemptuous.

"Like him . . . yes," she answered, her voice low, her chin and temper on the rise.

He stopped and took her arm, turning her into him so hard that the long tawny locks fell away from the top of her head and cascaded down her back in sudden freedom. She looked a beauty, a wild-spirited creature, and as he gazed his desire increased.

"Jewelene . . ." he said, his voice husky, "would you have him ruined? Go to him, and I swear he will be ruined! *I have the means.*"

She attempted to pull away from his embrace, but he held her pressed to him; his other arm was already about her, and her struggle only fed his hunger. She saw the light in his eyes and knew a moment of trepidation. Caesar, she thought at once, and called loudly for the dog. However, the Great Dane had rambled out of earshot, and Omsbury's mouth was already closing on hers.

"Ahem!" said a deep male voice at Jewelene's back. "It seems I have this lamentable habit of forever interrupting you, my lord!" said the marquess, his steel gray eyes meeting Omsbury's vicious glance.

Omsbury's voice spoke of war. "Indeed, sir! Your *habit*, as you call it, is beginning to wear thin on my good graces."

"Good graces? I wasn't aware that you possessed any," said the marquess, clenching his fists behind his back. He wished very much that Omsbury would make a move . . . any sort of move. He wanted an excuse to lay hands on him. However, Jewelene had now freed herself from Omsbury's grasp. Something sinister in Omsbury's threat frightened her to the very core. She had found herself alone and helpless with him, and then out of nowhere appeared this large ginger-haired, gray-eyed gambler, and her heart soared. All she knew was that he was shelter, and she ran to his side, pressing herself to him almost childlike.

Instinctively, his arm went round her shoulder, and his gloved fingers took up her chin as though to bolster her back into spirits. "You have a guest at the house, Jewelene. Mr. Clay has arrived. Shall I escort you back?"

"Oh, yes, yes, do," she breathed, her eyes meeting his thankfully.

He returned his attention to Omsbury. "You and I shall meet at another time, my lord, depend upon it!" With these ominous words he turned round and led Jewelene back to the house.

Ben Clay was ushered into the parlor where he was told Miss Elizabeth worked at her embroidery. He stood looking at her as she glided across the room, welcoming him with outstretched hand and a soft smile. Her eyes lowered before his, and it was very hard for her to tell herself he was for Jewelene, for her heart beat most outrageously against such knowledge.

"Miss Elizabeth . . . you are looking radiant," he said, his voice restrained, his forehead near to feverish.

She blushed. "Jewelene has gone out for a walk. May I offer you some refreshment while you wait?"

"No, you may offer me your company, since it is that I have come seeking."

She blushed a deeper shade and turned away. He misunderstood this to mean such compliments were unwelcome. He thought at once of his infirmity. She was disgusted by it. It was his turn to flush, to look away. But Elizabeth was a lady. It was unthinkable that such an uncomfortable situation should continue. "Mr. Clay . . . er . . . Jewelene tells me you are acquainted with the poet Keats."

"Oh . . . yes . . . but only slightly. We met during one of my turns in London," he said coming closer to her.

"I . . . I admire his poetry greatly . . . though he is much criticized," she said timidly, wondering why he wore such a stricken look. After a moment, she added, "Jewelene laughs to hear me praise him. She thinks there is no poet like her Byron!"

"She has a point there. Byron's life may be held in question, but there is such in his work that one must needs admire."

"Of course . . . you and Jewelene . . . would feel the same . . ." she stammered.

He frowned. "Why, of course?" He shook his head. "More times than not Jewelene and I disagree on everything from . . . from poetry to horses!"

"Really?" she said, much surprised. "I would think that . . . uncomfortable."

"Would you? I think it uncommon among friends but certainly not uncomfortable. But why must we speak of Jewelene? I did not come here for that," he said plunging into the heart of the matter.

"Did you not, sir?" she said, her voice soft in spite of her conscience.

"Elizabeth?" he said, his heart in his throat.

Jewelene still held firmly to the marquess's arm as they took the path back to the house. She was silent with her thoughts and he with his until finally it burst from him.

"I don't understand, Jewelene. Why the deuce don't you send the knave packing?"

"It is not so simple."

"Is it not? How so?" he asked, for he was determined to understand this chit.

"You see, I can do no more than I have . . . without bringing James into it, and that, sir, simply would not do. His youth equips him with many honorable ideals . . . he would feel obliged to call Lord Omsbury out! I love my brother. Do you think I would allow him to risk his life across a dueling field?"

The marquess frowned. "All right then . . . why allow yourself to be caught up with such a man in private . . . out here in the woods?"

She put up her chin, "Really, sir! This is Henshaw land. May I not walk on my own land? I had no notion he would come down upon me . . . and when he did . . . must I run back to the house like some sniveling child?"

"Yes, you must . . . for with such as he you are no more than that!" he answered harshly.

"Again, it is not so simple. You see, he has asked me to marry him, and I have promised to give him my answer in two weeks."

"What?" he ejaculated, "You would sell yourself to Omsbury?"

She was furious now. She didn't have to explain herself to this man simply because he chose to come along so opportunely.

"Have you not heard? I am something of an . . . ape-leader, a spinster, sir! I have not many chances left to me!"

He nearly choked, "You call marrying such a jackanapes a chance?"

"For myself, no . . . no . . . I loathe the very notion. But there are other considerations . . ."

"Do tell me about them?" he sneered. "The scoundrel has a handsome fortune, no doubt."

"Indeed he does . . . but 'tis not . . ."

"For what, then?" He turned on her fiercely. "Tell me what else he has to offer . . ."

"I . . . I . . . cannot . . ." she faltered. Then she saw the contempt in his eyes and lost her temper. How dare he? He was naught but a fortune-seeker himself . . . a libertine, making love to this one at one moment . . . another the next. Was he not the same man who had taken Babette in his arms last night? Now here he was spouting his moralities at her. It was the outside of enough! And then she was in his arms again and he was kissing her as he had the night before. She managed to yank herself out of his embrace and gasped, aware of the sensation he had aroused within her breast. But how dare he? How dare his eyes lie? And they did lie. Last night he had looked at Babette with something akin to this. *"You, you cad!"* she spat, "you . . . how dare you?" Her eyes raked him with their angry glitter.

He stared into their depths, and then he started with sudden sure knowledge. Her eyes! They were the same eyes. He could say nothing as he stood there, staring down at her angry little face.

She didn't notice his expression—she was too incensed at him. "You . . . you libertine . . . let me go!" she said, wrenching out of his hold and fleeing him.

He watched her go, still struck with his newfound knowledge.

"My God!" he breathed, "Jewelene . . . Babette . . ."

Fourteen

Sir James stood on the yawl and breathed the dirty air of Portsmouth's docks but seemed not in the least perturbed. He was on somewhat of an adventure and determined to approve of everything. Their horses and portmanteaux were already awaiting them, and they had but to make their way past the crowd. However, this they did with less dignity than Sir James had foreseen.

For some unexplained reason, Arthur began to spend more time casting his eyes about and behind than he did watching where he was going. Inevitably this resulted in a series of stumbles that nearly brought down both young men. However, Sir James let out a shout of desperation and flung out his arms, catching the wooden railing with his left hand and his friend with his right, thus saving them from a fall.

"Odds fish!" he ejaculated as he set himself to rights and stared down his friend. "What in the name of all . . . what is wrong with you, Art? Been fidgeting over something ever since we docked!"

"Don't know, Jimmy. Something is wrong . . . I feel it . . ." said Arthur, frowning.

"You feel it?" said Jimmy with a resigned and heavy sigh. "What exactly do you feel?"

"That's it! Don't know," answered his friend helplessly.

"Clunch!" said his friend. Arthur shuffled his feet but declined to argue, thinking perhaps, just perhaps, this abuse was not altogether unwarranted.

"Mount your horse," said Jimmy eyeing him after a moment.

"Right." Arthur felt this was something he could do without any further deviation. But then once again he got this dreadful tingling in the back of his neck. It was just as he put his foot in the stirrup that he turned just a trifle too sharply, causing his horse to whinny and jaunt about in the crowd. This in turn sent Jimmy's horse into a flurry, and it was some minutes before they had their animals righted and themselves firmly mounted in the saddle.

Sir James eyed Arthur Salford for a moment while he tried to compose his temper; however, he soon decided there was no need to so suffer and let loose an opprobrious harangue on his friend's lowered head. This he continued to do while they tooled their horses through the maze of traffic down the main thoroughfare, interrupting himself only once to ask Arthur the right direction.

It was some moments later that they found themselves in a section of the city that was less trafficked and also less worthy of them. Sir James looked over the decrepit buildings and eyed his friend with a sigh. " 'Tis a sad day indeed, Art . . . that I, a Henshaw, should be forced to such a deed!"

"Aye, they're not nice people, these *tens-in-the-hundred*!" remarked Arthur knowingly.

Sir James was seen to bolster himself as they drew up before the two-story brick building he was about to enter. "Well, nothing for it. It is the only thing that will fit."

"I'd rather be booked than have to sell my soul to a moneylender!" sighed Arthur. "You've got backbone, you have, Jimmy!"

Sir James called to a link boy and bade him watch their horses. "Come on, old friend. In we go."

"Lordy . . . if your sister ever finds out . . . egad!" Arthur had a terrible thought. "Proper in the suds we'll be!"

"Well, we'll just make certain she don't get wind of it!"

"And if she happens to notice the jewels missing?" said Arthur.

"She won't. She never bothers wearing jewelry . . . and I took only the very largest piece . . . now come on."

Thus, Sir James, with his staunch friend at his side, made his first visit to a moneylender. He sat there waiting for his prey, did this one, his beard reaching the desk and the money he counted there and his spectacles nearly falling off his long nose.

Outside, a wiry groom in a peaked cap and wool riding coat rubbed his stubbled chin. What would Sir James be doing at such a place? Visiting a moneylender. . . and one that was notorious for the interest rates he charged? He strolled out of sight and waited, for Lord Omsbury would want to know everything. It would be his job to continue to follow Sir James until he knew the whole!

Jewelene's honey tresses strayed all around her delicate shoulders, shoulders that shook with frustration and rage. She slammed the front door and took the stairs like a tigress on the attack. He . . . he was a cur, this gingerhaired libertine . . . this . . . this gamester! Well, he would soon learn to play with her . . . she would teach him a thing or two. But how, how? And then like a shaft of light it came to her. Of course! *Babette* . . . Babette could do the trick.

She sat on her bed much struck with this notion. Oh, thank goodness for Babette! Indeed, the Frenchwoman could do everything she could not. Babette could tease, entrance, entrap, and then strike him down for the detestable, arrogant profligate he was. And believing all this to be so, to be possible, she still felt somehow empty.

Belowstairs Ben and Elizabeth had finally discovered one another. However, they had heard Jewelene's mad dash, and Elizabeth had gone to the parlor door. She had seen Jewelene take the stairs like a woman demented and knew she must go to her cousin. She turned to Ben Clay. "Something has overset her . . . I must go up to her at once."

"Of course . . . and I must go to Yarmouth. I should not have stayed with you so long . . . while your mother was not at home . . ."

She smiled softly at him. He was so good, this great big warm-hearted man. Her heart felt full with the sure knowledge that his esteem for her matched hers for him. She went with him to the front door and gave him her hand. He bent low and long over it. "Elizabeth?" And then his eyes met hers once again drawing her breath out of her lungs.

"Good afternoon, sir," she managed. This was too much, too soon, and she had to be certain she did not betray her cousin. If Jewelene were to be hurt by this . . . she would withdraw.

He pulled himself up, but his voice came low, husky, heartfelt. "Until tomorrow, beloved." And then he was gone.

She stared after him awhile. *Beloved!* It rang in her ears, it tingled her spirits, it breathed life into her being. *Beloved!* It was such a word . . . such a word! She turned, resolutely putting it aside. She had to go to Jewelene.

Jewelene looked up at the sound of the knock and

called out, "Come in," but it was evident from the tone of her voice that she was in a black mood.

Elizabeth peeped in and Jewelene, seeing her cousin's expression of concern, gave over at once. "Why, Lizzie, love . . . what is it?"

Elizabeth laughed softly. "Isn't it just like you, Jewel, to put the very question to me that I had intended for you."

Jewelene smiled ruefully, "Ah, you heard my entrance. I am sorry, dear. I just couldn't help myself. 'Tis naught but a tantrum and not worth your indulgence."

"Nonsense, Jewel, you never have tantrums, so what is it—please? Can you not confide in me?"

"Oh, Liz, I am never one that can reveal my feelings easily. But if I ever did, 'twould be to you, darling, and well you know it."

"Is . . . is . . . it . . . Ben?" asked Elizabeth, her eyes clouding.

"Ben? Oh, that's right. Ben is here . . . did he wish to see me? I had quite forgotten he had come," said she.

Elizabeth's brows went up. That certainly did not sound like a lady in love. "No, actually . . . he has left . . ."

Jewelene looked up at her and frowned, "That is another thing."

"What is?" said Elizabeth, feeling that as usual she was losing control of the conversation. Jewelene always had a way of taking it over and sending it in the direction of her making.

"You and Ben, of course. We shall have to bring Aunt Dora about, but how we are to do it is beyond me at the moment," said Jewelene, putting a finger to her lips.

Elizabeth looked astonished and she blushed rosily.

"Ben . . . Ben . . . and I . . . but Jewelene . . . there is . . . no . . ."

"Oh, tush, Liz. Did you think I would not know? In truth . . . I did not until yesterday. But now that I do, why I will not rest until everything is set between you. I suppose Ben will have to sell the Silver Heart. I have thought and thought . . . and that really is the only solution . . . but how he is to derive a comfortable income if he does sell the Silver Heart . . . well . . . I just don't know!" pronounced Jewelene, more to herself than to her cousin.

The one thing that Elizabeth did understand from her cousin's ramblings was the fact that Jewelene did not appear to be in love with Ben Clay. And this was most startling, thought Elizabeth, considering the quality of the man, but there it was.

"Then you are not in love with Ben?" asked Elizabeth, evidently needing confirmation of her hopes.

Jewelene looked up at Elizabeth and gave a hoot of laughter. "Me . . . in love with . . . with Ben?"

This rather annoyed Elizabeth, and seeing this, Jewel continued:

"But Elizabeth . . . well, I see you don't understand the situation. You and he met as adults . . . you have not known him most of your life . . . thought of him as . . . something akin to an older brother . . . but I have!"

"Oh, oh, I see," Elizabeth brightened.

Jewelene sighed. For no particular reason she was feeling more the thing and so she said, "So, angel of mine, you have cheered my spirit, and the only thing I need now is some sleep."

Elizabeth touched her cousin's forehead. "Are you all right, love? I have never known you to take a nap during the day."

"I am quite all right . . . just tired. I didn't sleep well last night. 'Tis all this excitement . . . with the race coming up in a week . . ." she faltered, looking away. She hated deceiving the people she loved. But it was after all for their own good.

So Jewelene was left to her pillows and after a time she dozed off. But her rest was not peaceful. Her dreams made her toss, and when the time ticked by she did not wake rested. It was Lyla's giggling that made her lids open, but it was Keith's voice that set her jaw. She could hear his low masculine voice in the hall and though she could not make out the words, her imagination filled them in, for no sooner had Keith stopped speaking than Lyla began giggling again.

Keith had stood dumbfounded with his discovery before he was able to move and follow her to the house and, when he did arrive, it was to pass Ben Clay. He liked Clay but his eyes glinted angrily at him as he paused, one leg raised to the step. "Mr. Clay! You and I have something to discuss!" he said sternly.

"Do we?" said Clay surprised. "I can't imagine what, but I am ready, sir, whenever you wish."

"Good. Come along then," said the marquess walking away from the house, his hands clasped behind his back. "It is about Miss Henshaw."

"Oh?" said Clay carefully.

"Indeed, sir . . . you consider yourself her friend?"

"I do."

"Then may I ask why you are allowing this charade of hers?" asked the marquess, his brow up, his eyes hard.

Ben Clay sighed. Well then, this man knew. "What do you mean to do?"

"You haven't answered my question, sir!" retorted the marquess harshly.

"And you, sir, concern yourself in matters better left alone," said Clay. "You do not know Miss Henshaw well enough to understand . . ."

"I understand that what you are allowing her to do could very well ruin her! She must think she has very good reasons . . . I know that much of her . . . but you sir, you know better!"

"Yes, I do . . . but if I had not lent her my services . . . she might very well have taken Omsbury!" snapped Clay.

The marquess frowned and said nothing for a moment. Then, "Why? What is the desperation here?"

"It is not for *me* to discuss with *you*," said Clay.

"Oh, is it not?" sneered the marquess. "I don't know what sort of game you are all playing, but I mean to find out."

"Why? What has it got to do with you?" asked Ben, somewhat annoyed.

The marquess glared at him a moment but found he had no answer to this. He dodged the question instead, "Because, sir, something smoky is going on, and I owe it to my hostess to see to it that she is not thrown into scandal . . . or are you forgetting Mrs. Debbs?"

"No, no, how could I . . ." faltered Ben Clay. "I mean to marry her daughter!"

"You mean to marry Elizabeth Debbs?" ejaculated the marquess incredulously. "Why, that is beyond everything the finest piece of news yet!"

"Is it?" Ben was surprised at the man's jubilation.

"Well, then . . . good day to you . . . and mind, not

a word to Jewelene about our little talk. I hold you honor-bound," said the marquess.

"You don't mean to let her go on . . . not knowing . . . *you* know?"

"I do. Trust me . . . I mean her no harm. Quite the opposite, in fact."

Ben Clay did trust him, and he rode away feeling that things just might turn out all right, if only Jewelene would not discover she had been found out. For if that little miss learned she was being duped . . . oh, God! there was no thinking what she might do.

Fifteen

"Well, you shouldn't wear it ... makes you look a coxcomb!" said Sir James, shaking his head.

"No? Really, Jimmy, that is too bad of you," returned Arthur, feeling his friend had gone too far. " 'Tis the highest kick of fashion!"

"No, it isn't ... at least ... not in *that* quantity and manner! I mean, just look at all that stuffing," said Sir James, casting his eyes disparagingly over Arthur's shoulders. "Ain't seemly, Art, really give you m'word. Look at my shoulders ... you don't see me using all that buckram and wadding!"

"Well, 'tis easy for you, Jimmy. You ain't condemned to round shoulders. *I am!* Don't like m'shoulders to stoop. Buckram and wadding fixes that right and tight!"

Sir James shook his head, but something else had taken hold of his attention. They approached a milestone indicating that Trowbridge was some fifty miles ahead. He frowned, remembering something from his youth, and halted his horse. "Trowbridge?" he said softly to himself. Then to his companion, "Odd that ... are you sure we are heading in the right direction?"

"Of course. Read the guide, didn't I?"

"Hmm ... here, give it over a moment," said Sir James, reaching.

He scanned the map with his finger tracing a line before he gave a disgusted exclamation. "Clunch! What is it? Midsummer moon with you? We are heading in the wrong direction. We should have taken the fork toward Swindon!"

"But I was careful to read the guide most thoroughly," said Arthur, casting puppylike eyes on his friend.

"Aye, with the map folded so that the line you traced was false. Dolt! If ever there was such a noddy . . . good Lord, Art . . . how you manage to get by? Well, come on then, we'll have to retrace our steps!"

"Well, happen it's a good thing," said Arthur thoughtfully.

He got rapped with the guidebook for such a statement. "A good thing? Are you jesting?"

"No, I am not. I know you haven't taken me seriously . . . and I admit I haven't seen anything, but, Jimmy, I do get this very odd sensation down the back of my neck . . . I believe we are being followed."

"Do you, moonling? If ever there was such a zany . . ."

"But, Jimmy, don't you see? Turning back unexpectedly like this, well, we'll know, won't we?"

Jimmy eyed him for a moment. "Art, never say you made us go the wrong way simply to test your theory?"

"No, no. Never thought of it. Not needle-witted like you, but seems to be . . . expedient."

Jimmy threw up his hands as they began retracing their steps.

Babette moved restlessly across the E.O. chamber, her gold silks rustling about her. Gold stars were affixed to her raven locks, but her neck was bare of ornaments. The room was filling, and she smiled greetings to the men entering, but she waited for but one man. Oh, when she thought of the audacity of him at dinner that very evening. He was *insufferable*.

He had behaved as though nothing had passed between them, as though Jewelene had no cause to be so cold to him, and he had flirted outrageously with her. It had brought his cousin the marquess's head round with wonder several times, and Lyla . . . the little snide remarks she had had to endure from that chit. Well, he would pay!

He came in presently, his cousin beside him, and she watched him, an odd little smile playing about her painted lips. She met his gaze and waited for him to come to her.

"Babette, my beauty," he said sweetly. "You have no notion how dull the day has been without you."

She seethed, but said softly. "Ah, for me too . . ."

His brow went up in spite of himself. He meant to tease her, play with her. His new-found knowledge gave him an edge, but her sudden willingness to flirt with him came as a surprise.

Omsbury appeared at the chamber doorway. His eyes scanned the room carelessly, stopping to meet those of the marquess in mock greeting. Babette's breath quickened as did her heartbeat, her hand reached out and touched Keith's, and again he was reminded of a frightened child. He had a strong sudden urge to comfort her, to take her in his arms, and put all her fears to rest.

She whispered as though trying to catch her breath, "Ah, m'sieur . . . if you please . . . could we perhaps move away from here?"

Knowing it was Omsbury sending her into such a fret, he patted her gloved hand, "Of course, love. You are wise not to invite the attentions of *that one!*" he said meaningfully.

"What mean you . . . which one?" she returned, thinking herself very clever.

He put up a brow. Playful, was she? Very well, he too could play. Though, in truth, it wasn't really fair. "Why I was speaking of Omsbury, but it seems I err. Shall I bring him round? I had not realized you might desire an introduction."

She clung to his arm as though to ward off a blow, "No, no!"

Again he patted her hand, "I thought not. A wise decision, my love, for he is a dangerous fellow. But come, let us not speak of him, let us speak of us . . . where can we be alone?"

"Alone? But I have the faro."

"Jem can deal for a time, and you and I must talk," he said firmly.

"Of course . . . if it is your wish, then I must hold it to be mine as well," she agreed, her eyes flashing bewitchingly. The look she gave him nearly took his breath away. It was full of promise of things to come. Whatever was she up to? He said slowly, "My wish? Indeed it has been my wish to be alone with you from the first moment we met."

"Ah, but I fear you sadly deceive me, sir. *You,* I am persuaded, have many women who . . . interest you?" she baited.

"No, Babette . . . only one," he said truthfully, though a twinkle lit his gray eyes.

Oh, it was too much, really! How dare he lie so . . . so bare-facedly, she thought angrily. Throwing caution to the winds, she said, "But Ben . . . he tells me you stay at the Henshaw House . . . *oui?*"

"Y . . . es," he answered, pretending to hesitate.

"And zair lives . . . a young woman?"

"Two . . . discounting Mr. Clay's sister," he answered glibly.

"And these two women . . . neither finds favor in your eyes?" she asked sweetly.

"Oh, as to that . . . perhaps Miss Henshaw might be considered by some to be something of a beauty . . . but . . . ah, Babette . . . what is she to you?"

"Indeed!" snapped Babette, not at all pleased.

"Why, what have I said, darling?" he asked, all innocence.

They had by then reached the end of the long corridor that led to Ben Clay's office. Keith's hand had been resting on the knob; he opened the door and eased her within.

"Tell me . . ." said Jewelene, spinning round to face him, noting that he had closed the door and frowning slightly over this, "you say . . . she . . . this Henshaw woman . . ."

"Child," he corrected.

She controlled herself and inclined her head though her eyes betrayed her. "Child, then! She attracts you not?"

The corner of his mouth quivered. "Does it so matter to you, my love?"

"But *oui* . . . how could it not? I . . . la, none knows better than I how beneath you is my birth . . ."

"It doesn't matter. It is not as though I am heir to a title. I have a brother whose children are before me."

"Yes, but this Henshaw . . . er . . . child. She is of your class?"

"Let us not speak of her, my love, when it is you who enchant me," he said, winding his arms round her.

She disengaged herself neatly and could not restrain her foot from tapping on the carpet. "Ah, you wish to kiss me . . . but me, I think it is she you kiss by day?"

"As a matter of fact, love, I did kiss her and found her sorely lacking your charms . . ." he said suavely.

"You . . . you did? Sorely . . . lacking?" hissed Babette. "I . . . I think now I will return to my table, *oui*!" with which she sped from the room and left him to his chuckles. He was enjoying this far more than was decent.

It was nearly dusk when Sir James and Art began retracing their way to the point where they had taken a wrong turn.

It was an unfamiliar route, and the declining sun allowed some irregular shades to be cast by the overhanging trees. A breeze came up, and Sir James began to feel something—he was not quite certain just what it was. However, being a practical-minded fellow he shrugged it off and looked with some annoyance at his friend. "There!" he said all at once after a long interim of silence. "You've got me spooked!"

Arthur was listening though. He had heard something, something that made him bring his reins in and his horse to a complete halt. Sir James turned round and eyed him. "What in thunder?" with which he stopped as well. Thus they stood. After a moment Sir James poohed their silliness away. " 'Tis naught, Art. Just someone approaching on horseback."

"Aye . . . so it is . . . and much like I said," Arthur's voice was ominous.

Sir James's expression became grim, and his gloved hand moved to a horse pistol at his saddle. "All right then, let him come . . ."

But no one came. They waited for they had both heard the unmistakable sounds of an approaching rider. However, the wait was in vain.

It was not that Jenkins had given up his task. Indeed, no. However, as they had heard him, so had he heard them. He slid off his horse, walked the steed into the thicket and proceeded to stalk on foot. He half suspected the gentlemen he was trailing had doubled back, and Jenkins was ever a sly one. And so he waited for them to proceed before mounting his horse and taking up the chase once again.

Dark was soon upon them, and Arthur suggested as he saw the beckoning lights of a posting house, "What say you, Jimmy? Shall we call it a day and get an early start tomorrow morning?"

"Yes, and you know, Art . . . I am beginning to think you are right. Something strange is going on. I feel it too. Perhaps we should situate ourselves tonight, and perhaps we should then have a look about . . . safer if we know our grounds."

"Aye," agreed his friend.

"Oh, Ben . . . will they never go home?" cried Jewelene taking him aside. She was no longer dealing faro. It was past three already, supper had been consumed, and most of the players were departing in small groups, but the marquess and his cousin showed no signs of leaving the E.O. table.

"You will just have to precede them tonight," said Ben, frowning, wondering what Keith was about.

"Very well. I shall just run over to your house and change into my breeches. Meet me down the street with the horses, Ben," she said slipping out of the gaming room.

The marquess had been watching her from the corner of his eye. Indeed, he had been hovering possessively about her all night, shielding her for the most part from Omsbury. He meant to deal with Omsbury himself, but first he had to keep that man from discovering what was afoot. This seemed easy enough as Omsbury's eyes rarely strayed to the raven-haired beauty.

In the meantime, the marquess was thoroughly amused by the situation that prevailed. He had no intention of allowing it to continue very much longer as he had begun to have very definite plans for Jewelene Henshaw, but for the time being he was rather curious to see how she would attempt to bring herself about. It was this that caused him to linger with Robby, forcing her hand. For one thing he wanted to see just how she had been getting in and out of the house without disturbing anyone.

He had no sooner seen Jewelene leave and Ben follow then he was tugging at Robby's sleeve. "Come on, coz, shake your shambles! We must leave."

Robby stared in some surprise. The marquess had not yet told his cousin about the new and most interesting developments. He soon found himself being dragged along unceremoniously, his cloak being slung carelessly about his shoulders, his top hat plumped without concern on his head. Even an amiable nature gets ruffled now and then and so he advised his cousin all the way down the stairs, and over the cobblestones to the stables, and then over the cobbles again. All at once the whirlwind at his side had stopped, and Rob ceased his harangue to gaze about him in wonder.

"Why are we hiding in this filthy passage?"

"Shh . . . now if only our horses may not give us away," whispered the marquess at his side.

Robby narrowed his eyes and stuck out his head the better to view his cousin. "You all right, old friend?"

"Sh-h . . . I said," returned Keith impatiently.

"Sh-h? Yes, to be sure . . . sh-h," said Robby deciding Keith needed humoring.

Then they saw Ben leading two horses to the street corner. Clay had no sooner taken up his stand when he was joined by a small figure enveloped in a dark, hooded cloak. They watched the two figures mount and vanish down the street.

"Now, Robby . . . now we shall see!" said the marquess with a wide grin.

"Yes, of course, splendid, old boy," returned Robby, wondering what maggot had entered his cousin's head. Why the deuce should Keith wish to follow the owner of the Silver Heart? Clearly this trip to the Isle of Wight had done strange things to the Marquess of Lyndhurst.

Sixteen

The marquess had sent Rob to the Henshaw stables with their horses, urging him to proceed to his room and bidding him good-night. Of his own intentions he would not speak, but proceeded forthwith on foot round the large rambling house to observe, just in the nick of time, as the saying goes, Jewelene, cloak over one arm, scrambling up the trellis to her window ledge.

He smiled to himself. She was really up to every necessity, and then a wicked notion came to mind. He rushed to the front door, to which both he and Robby had been given keys, crossing the marble hall with lightninglike speed, and took the stairs two at a time to Jewelene's door. There he stopped a moment before knocking rather soundly on its wooden frame.

On the other side stood Jewelene, her clothes at her feet, her nightdress but half on. She gasped but called out in what she hoped was a sleepy voice, "Y–es?"

"Miss Jewelene! It is I, Keith . . . open your door at once. I fear there is a prowler making for your window!" hissed the marquess.

Oh, no! He must have come home in time to witness me climbing up my own trellis. Well, there was nothing for it but to allow him to search. She only hoped he would not bring down the entire house about their ears. "Just a moment," she said, grabbing a white satin wrapper and slipping this over her nightdress. She was still attempting to tie the sash when she opened the door wide and stood aside allowing him to enter. He came, all in a rush, sweeping past her so that she stared in utter amazement. They had but the moon and the candle he held in his hand for light. The candle he put down on a near-by table as he reached the closed window, opened it, and looked out.

"Gone! The devil! He was making for your room, Jewelene. Rob and I must have frightened him off when we arrived." He turned to her, his eyes all concern for her well-being. "But you are quite safe . . . no one disturbed you?"

"No one but you, sir," she said haughtily. She could still hear him tell Babette what a child Jewelene was.

He came toward her, taking off his kid gloves, and she was watching him, wondering what now he intended when he pointed a finger at her. So quick was the action that she didn't think to draw back. Too late she saw the expression of distaste on his face. "You look, Jewelene, even at this hour, a stunning creature, though I cannot think this red on your lips does you credit!"

Oh, drat! she thought, the paint . . . I am still wearing Babette's paint! She offered lamely, " 'Tis . . . 'tis . . . a salve to . . . er . . . heal this chapping I have had trouble with of late."

"Very good," he applauded.

She opened her wide eyes wider, much startled at his response, and was about to remark upon the singularity of it when he added blandly, "Very good indeed. I understand such things work wonders overnight. . . though it might rub off on your pillow." He was already far too close to her, she thought, as she gazed up into his twinkling eyes.

He had very properly left her hall door wide open, but she felt it prudent to dismiss him all the same. "Do you not think it time you allowed me to return to my bed?"

He looked from her to this handsome structure and then back again in such a way that her every nerve tingled. She blushed, waiting for him to do, to say, something and then at last he sighed, "Indeed . . . child, I bid thee good night." He took up her hand and placed there a lingering kiss. She withdrew it sharply, far more sharply than Babette had done some hours ago. But he merely smiled, touched her chin as he drew up to his full height, and said on a parting note, "Sweet dreams, my love," and was gone.

She stood seething. "Of all the gall, the arrogant, cocksure, libertine flirt! By God! I will bring him to his knees if I can!"

Sir James and Arthur engaged rooms for the night. However, while these were being prepared, they lingered in the tavern. No one of any particular note entered, and they soon forgot their suspicions and settled down to a convivial evening.

"Where ye gents be headed?" asked the tavernkeeper, placing another round of ale before his guests.

"Derby," offered Arthur amiably. "Mean to enter a horse there."

"You don't say! Be it prime blood then . . . a thoroughbred . . . Welsh?"

"Lord, no!" sniffed Arthur. "He's a Spanish stallion. A handsome devil . . . mean to breed him after he downs them all."

Sir James had risen from the round table and moved to the arched entrance. Something, a shadow? . . had caught his eye. It hovered, neither coming nor going. As he arrived at the arch, he pounced round with an excited sound only to find that his quarry had eluded him. Quick-witted, Jimmy rushed down the hall and into the courtyard in time to see a small wiry man ride past him on horseback. A peaked cap was pulled low over the little scoundrel's face, but Jimmy recognized him all the same. "Jenkins!" he said in a soft, worried voice, "Jenkins . . . now what would Omsbury's man be doing here?"

Arthur, tankard of ale in hand, had followed Sir James. He came up behind him now, "What's toward, Jimmy . . . you took off like a bull!"

"You were right all along, Arthur . . . damn if you weren't!"

"Was I?" said Arthur, much pleased. "Is that good?" he asked, after worrying over it a moment.

"I don't know. It all depends on how much he has learned and what he means to do with it," responded Sir James.

"Does it? Who . . . what?"

"Come along inside. I doubt that you'll be *feeling* any more odd sensations down the back of your neck, you old sorcerer!"

Arthur took this as high flattery indeed, and they went in, much pleased with one another for the time being.

Lyla shook her head over a length of material and moved down the narrow aisle to a roll of red that caught her eye. It was spangled with beads throughout, and she exclaimed delightedly over it. "Elizabeth, do look . . . how superb!"

Liz cast a glance her way and then heavenward. "No Lyla, it won't do!" She had already made her selection and was anxious to proceed, for they were to meet with Jewelene across the street to pick out ribbons.

"Why won't it do? I daresay my mother would just

adore it for me. She has already told me that red suits me quite well, thank you," she was pouting.

"But Lyla . . . I am certain she did not mean all reds and certainly not one with beads throughout. It is quite vulgar, I do assure you."

"Oh, very well then, let us go for I am not in the mood to continue anyway!" said Lyla, pushing past Miss Debbs and going outdoors.

Elizabeth followed her, patiently trying to keep up a friendly conversation, until they were forced to stop before a tall, distinguished, somehow devilishly attractive older man. Lord Omsbury made them his bow. Lyla cast admiring eyes over him and dimpled prettily, attempting to engage his attention, but he seemed intent on speaking to Elizabeth.

"I am so pleased to meet you, Miss Debbs. I have been so wanting to speak to you about your cousin," he said softly.

Elizabeth did not like him, he frightened her and she knew too well how Jewelene loathed him. She put up her chin, "I can't imagine what we could talk about in her absence, my lord."

"Very worthy of you, but not very wise. Your cousin seems determined to set her cap for a man who plays false with her."

"I . . . I don't know what you mean," said Elizabeth.

"I am speaking of Mr. Clay," said his lordship, smiling apologetically at Miss Clay who opened her eyes wide with astonishment.

"You mistake the matter," said Elizabeth, thinking now she understood.

"Do I? I don't think so. I rarely do . . . make mistakes. Mr. Clay has made it known that his heart and in all probability his hand goes to a Frenchwoman . . . a gaming wench who works at his faro table in the Silver Heart!"

Elizabeth's hand went involuntarily to her heart. It wasn't true. He lied. For some devious reason of his own he lied. But Lyla tittered, "Oh, gracious! So that's what those dratted stableboys were whispering about. They said she wears a mask and no one knows who she is."

"Exactly so. I hope you will take my warning in good stead and see to it that Miss Henshaw is not allowed to be hurt in this regard." He moved away. "Good day, ladies."

"Why, there is Ben now . . . only wait till I tease him!" cried Lyla. "Ben . . . Ben . . ."

Elizabeth felt her heart shrivel within her breast, her mouth was dry, and her throat constricted. Under such discomfort, it was very difficult to raise her eyes to those of Ben Clay's and thus she missed the look of adoration he cast her way.

"Ben, you naughty boy!" laughed Lyla, but spying a girl friend across the square she hurried off saying she would be back in a moment.

Ben Clay moved closer to his love. His beloved jerked back as though he were some monster. "Don't touch me!" she breathed.

"What? What?" He saw Omsbury moving down the street. "What has that scoundrel been saying to you and Lyla?"

"You dare to call him a scoundrel . . . you . . . you . . . oh . . . I never want to see you again!" spat Elizabeth, no longer quiet, no longer gentle or soft, and she sped across the square to the trimming shop.

Jewelene looked up from her purchases, and her smile faded immediately. "Elizabeth! Darling. . . what is it?"

she said going forward, putting a comforting hand round her cousin's shoulder.

Mrs. Haber, the shopowner, clucked her tongue. "You look that pale, dearie, come . . . let me get you a spot of tea."

"No, no, Mrs. Haber, I . . . I think 'tis time I returned home, I am not feeling very well."

"Yes, Mrs. Haber, please don't bother yourself," said Jewelene, realizing whatever it was, Elizabeth needed privacy. "Come on, love, I'll see you home. Ben can bring Lyla home whenever she finishes her business in town." She led her cousin outdoors to their waiting curricle and bundled her inside the open carriage. Picking up the reins she executed a neat turnabout and made their way to Henshaw House, taking the main post road.

"Now Liz . . . what happened?"

"I . . . I know you mean well, Jewelene . . . but I don't want to talk about it . . . please," said Elizabeth on a sob.

"Oh, I think I understand. We will leave it for now . . . but later, Elizabeth, if you haven't settled it in your own head, we will talk!"

Elizabeth looked away.

In town Ben stalked down his sister and took her aside.

"Now, little girl, what was Omsbury saying to you two?"

"Oh, wouldn't you like to know . . . you great big lover, you."

"What mean you by that?"

"I didn't think any brother of mine would . . . after fighting the French and losing an arm to them . . . take up with one . . ." she sallied.

He went white. "Is that what Omsbury told you?"

"It is," she said.

"Stay here!" he said, stalking off.

"Where are you going?"

"To get the carriage and take you to Henshaw House."

"But I'm not ready to return yet, Benny . . . please . . ."

"Then get ready!" he snapped as he left her with her friend. He was in a wild fury. That Omsbury should say such a thing to a gently bred female was beyond anything, but that Elizabeth would believe it . . . turn against him without hearing him. It infuriated him to passion, strong bedeviled passion! He meant to have it out with her, now!

Some time later, Lord Omsbury sat meditatively in his library wing chair. From where he sat he had a majestic view of his rear courtyard and the sea beyond. He was by nature a town fellow, given to excesses, and though he had a rather strong feeling both for his family estate and heritage, he never liked remaining at Wight more than a month or so. However, things had changed. He had fallen in love. Oh, to be sure, his first blush of youth was gone and with it that idyllic fantasy one is prone to associate with love. Nevertheless, his heart beat now for but one woman—Jewelene.

He was a man used to having his own way. He envisioned a life with Jewelene. She would do his name honor. She would bear him children, many healthy, lusty children and, oddly enough, Lord Omsbury wanted children. A not unusual circumstance, his desire for an heir. He was after all approaching forty and was as we have said proud of his heritage. He meant for it to continue. His days of bachelordom must come to an end. Thus, he looked about for a wife, and there before his very eyes was a dream. Jewelene! He had met her at a small supper. With her informal address and easy manners, she enchanted him. He watched her laugh, move, talk, and found himself aware —all too aware—of her. She was beautiful, she was both child and woman—and he wanted her.

But the chit had notions of her own. He could not like her the less for them. In fact he admired her. She had everything to gain by giving him her hand. Her brother would go on to the university. She would gain a lovely home, a title, wealth. But she would not be bought, and that he liked. He had no doubt that given time and freedom, he could seduce her heart. He was an accomplished lover. But the headstrong chit would have to be forced. So be it. He liked the challenge.

Hence, he set out to win Jewelene. But he had no time for a long courtship. He was a ruthless man who took what he wanted. He would not go begging. That was for puppies in their first youth. Thus, he cogitated in the privacy of his elegant room, for he was bringing things to a climax, one of his own design and soon, soon she would have to concede the fight fairly won.

His butler interrupted his quiet by announcing Jenkins, and Omsbury's fine brow went up as the groom sauntered in. Omsbury took out a small enamel snuffbox and with his thumb and forefinger took an infinitesimal pinch. As he sniffed delicately he said, his voice level, "So, you are back, Jenkins? What news have you brought me?"

"Gawks, m'lord, you'll barely credit it!" ejaculated Jenkins, playing with the peaked cap in his hands. "I did as ye bid me, and hang me if Sir James and that friend of his didn't put to in Portsmouth Harbor, jest as ye said they would. . . ."

"I am fully cognizant of what I said, Jenkins. Do but confine your eloquence to the things I did not say."

"Aye . . . well then, Sir James and that friend of his took to horse and went straightaway . . . to a *tens-in-the-hundred!*" This he said with respectful awe for the expression to him was synonymous with the devil.

"A moneylender?" Omsbury was moved to ejaculate. "The young fool! He works against his sister in this. But what else, for I can see by your expression there is more."

"Aye, so there be, for I followed them still and they got right back on their mounts and took to the post road. I come to learn that they be headed for Derby to enter that 'orse of his. Thought you'd want me to come right back and tell you . . ."

Omsbury smiled. "You did well, Jenkins." He took a key and went across to his writing desk, unlocked a drawer and produced a wad of bills. "So . . . they intend to use borrowed money on which he will have to pay a wild interest rate to enter that stallion of theirs . . ." and then an idea came to mind and his eyes narrowed. "Well, well."

Seventeen

Jewelene and Elizabeth entered the house to find Mrs. Debbs in the parlor awaiting their return. Elizabeth turned to Jewel in the hallway and clasped her gloved hands, "Jewel . . . Jewel, I just can't face mother now . . . say I was tired after our shopping, nothing more. I don't want to be fussed over."

"Indeed, I shall do what is necessary, depend upon it. Now go on up and rest . . . and Lizzie . . . if I can help . . ."

"You are a dear," said Elizabeth, squeezing her hand and then making a dash for the stairs.

Jewelene, frowning, watched her a moment before sighing and turning to the closed parlor door. She went in and found Aunt Dora at her stitching. Idly she wondered where the marquess and his cousin were, "Hello, Auntie . . . all alone?"

"Oh hello, love. Yes, quite alone. The marquess announced his intention of riding over to Newport this afternoon where he has some acquaintances staying. It seems he met them in a tavern the other night. Gentlemen are always on such easy terms with one another . . . it makes things very pleasant for them."

"I suppose his cousin . . . accompanied him?" said Jewelene dropping her straw bonnet, gloves, and spencer on a nearby stool.

"No, Mr. Robendale remained behind. He is in the library reading. Such a nice young man . . . and so very handsome, though it wouldn't do to form a tendre in that direction, I do assure you, my girl. A second son is hardly qualified to provide the sort of living I desire for you."

The marquess had heard Jewelene's arrival and gave her just enough time, he thought, to get settled. He then rose and made his way to the parlor. Here he overheard Mrs. Debbs's remark and paused, waiting for Jewelene's answer.

"Oh, as to that, Auntie, I wouldn't give a fig for a man's living if I held him in esteem. What are such things?"

"My dear girl . . . oh, I don't suppose it would be any use to speak to you about comforts, for you are much the same as your mother!"

"Good afternoon, ladies," said a male voice at their back.

In spite of herself, Jewelene's heart began stirring. She raised her eyes to his, then lowered her lashes, veiling her thoughts as well.

"Did you enjoy your shopping expedition, Jewelene?" asked Keith.

"Yes, thank you." Drat the man, thought Jewelene, why did he cause the air to leave her lungs? Why did she suddenly become almost speechless?

"And you, sir?" put in Aunt Dora, "have you spent a pleasant morning among the books?"

"Indeed, yes, you have an excellent library here, but I think now I shall just get a bit of fresh air. I have been meaning to watch your Jonas put that horse of yours through his paces. He advised me yesterday that if I came up to the west field just about this hour, I would be in time for that very treat. I didn't want to leave, however, without bidding you a pleasant afternoon," he said, turning once more to the door.

He had baited the hook well. Would she bite? He moved slowly, hoping, his nerves tingling with anticipation, and when Jewelene's voice halted him, he felt much gratified.

"Keith . . . Mr. Robendale . . . I was myself going up to Lightning. If you will but wait for me to fetch my brother's timepiece . . ."

"Oh, as to that, I carry one . . . no need for you to get another," he offered politely.

She picked up her spencer, shrugged herself into its soft blue folds, pulled on her gloves, and held her bonnet by its blue ribbon, "Very well then, shall we go?" She turned to her aunt and blew her a kiss. "See you later, Auntie."

"Yes, dear. But where is Elizabeth?"

"Oh, Lyla wearied her as did the shopping. She is just lying down for awhile. She'll be down later."

"All right then . . . don't stay out too late, for there is no saying if the weather may take a bad turn," said Aunt Dora.

Jewelene smiled to herself thinking, neat auntie, very neat. As good a method as any of telling her to mind the proprieties.

The wind had taken on a briskness, and Jewelene glanced at Keith's open riding jacket as she pulled her own closed. "My goodness, I do hope we are not to have a storm." She was already worrying about the evening, wondering how she would contrive in the rain.

He smiled to himself for he was thinking very much the same. However, at this moment they spotted Ben Clay marching his sister down the lane that led from the stables. Jewelene waved as she and Keith drew up before them. "Hello Ben . . . my goodness! Whatever is wrong? You look as mad as Ajax!"

"Where is Elizabeth?" he said, his tone one Jewelene had never before heard.

"Inside . . . resting," said Jewelene hesitantly.

He tipped his hat to her, nodded to the marquess and, pulling his protesting sister along, proceeded to the house.

Jewelene stared after him for a long moment before a slow amused smile curved her lips.

"What entertains you, love?" asked the marquess, watching her.

"Much . . . and don't call me love!" she returned.

Inside, Ben turned to his sister as they were shown to the parlor and announced, "Now remember, I don't want what Omsbury told you repeated—not even in jest!"

"All right, Benny . . . I wouldn't do anything to so distress you. I am certain if I had known it would so put you out I would not have said a word to you," pouted the chit.

"As it turns out, it is just as well." He smiled at Mrs. Debbs and bowed over her extended hand.

"Why, Mr. Clay, how nice of you to bring Lyla to us and quite naughty of Elizabeth and Jewelene not to have waited for her to finish her business in town."

"It was no trouble, madam, I enjoy the ride to Henshaw. I wonder if I may beg an audience with your daughter. There is a matter I would discuss with her," said Ben taking the bull by the horns.

Mrs. Debbs hesitated. Really, this was something new. Whatever could Ben Clay want with Elizabeth? She was far too polite to refuse. "Of course," she said moving to the bellpull and summoning a lackey.

They waited, passing idle conversation until the lackey

had reappeared with the message that Miss Elizabeth would not see Mr. Clay.

Embarrassed, Mrs. Debbs blushed for her daughter. "I . . . I am sorry, Mr. Clay . . . my daughter did wish to rest this afternoon. Perhaps tomorrow . . ."

He was angry, but what could he do without creating a scene? Then too he was hurt. How could Elizabeth so misjudge him?

"Thank you," he said quietly, bowing once again. He turned to his sister. "Lyla," and then he was gone.

Mrs. Debbs watched his withdrawal and thought these proceedings spelled something, something she could not condone. "Lyla, will you excuse me dear? I think I will just go look in on Elizabeth."

Lyla frowned. Here she was . . . alone. Jewelene off with that handsome Keith Robendale. But that didn't matter. He was naught but a gamester with little means. The marquess was gone somewhere . . . her brother, it would seem, was in love with Elizabeth, though he had some French gaming wench on the side . . . and *she,* Lyla Clay, had no one! Then she thought of the older, handsome Lord Omsbury and sighed. He was titled, though to be sure he was but a baron, while Robby was a marquess . . . but Omsbury was so worldly, so handsome . . . and Lyla Clay sat down and began to plan.

They were crossing the field, but the road to Yarmouth was visible from where they stood atop the crest among tall waving grass. Jewelene's brows drew together as she spotted Ben Clay in his curricle, leaving by the private drive from her home.

"He seems a bit put out," remarked Keith.

"Yes, a lovers' quarrel, no doubt," answered Jewelene

lightly. Now that she knew what was toward, she would simply go and face Elizabeth and see just what those two silly creatures had fought about.

"Lovers' quarrel?" he returned, showing some surprise. "Do you mean Ben Clay and your cousin?" He meant to have some fun.

"Why, yes. Is it so surprising?"

"As a matter of fact, yes. Yes, it is. I had reason to believe Mr. Clay was interested in . . . someone else."

She frowned. Did he mean her or Babette? "In whom?" she asked.

"A . . . a woman *you* would not know. Yes, come to think of it, I seem to remember his advising me that he was betrothed to this . . . other woman."

"Well, it isn't true!" she snapped. Lord, if such a thing were carried back to Elizabeth!

He appeared very grave, "Ah, this is something I cannot like. Evidently you believe . . . indeed, I must assume that Clay has given you reason to believe that he is free to court Miss Debbs, while I know that is not true." He sighed and put up a hand stopping her from uttering a word. "I feel it is my duty to inform Miss Debbs regarding this circumstance."

"You wouldn't dare!" hissed Jewelene.

"But . . . I don't understand your attitude. The man takes unfair advantage."

"He does not. I . . . I know all about this other woman. He told me . . . and she is not . . . not connected to him romantically. He . . . he thinks about her as . . . as a . . . sister . . . yes, a sister."

"But . . . the man told me . . ."

"Yes, he told me about that incident . . . rather . . . I mean . . . he told me that this woman . . . the one of whom you speak. Well, that she she wished the men at the Silver Heart to . . . cease their unwanted attentions, hence . . . he gave them to believe . . ."

"Ah, that indeed must be it and just as I thought," said the marquess gravely.

"Just as you thought?" she asked feeling rather ill.

"Indeed yes . . . but there, is that not Jonas with Lightning?" He pointed, changing the subject. He had Jewelene and Babette just where he wanted them both . . . cornered.

Mrs. Debbs knocked softly at her daughter's door, once, twice, three times, before she was answered and then not very encouragingly.

"Go away," said the girl inside, sounding not at all like her habitually gentle self.

Her mother's brow went up. "But, dearest . . . 'tis mother."

"Oh," said Elizabeth, raising herself up. She hurriedly wiped her tearstained cheeks and tried to control her trembling lip. "Oh, yes . . . come in, mother."

Mrs. Debbs was frowning as she entered. Not that the estimable lady was angry at such a cold greeting from her child. The frown stemmed from a growing conviction that her only child was showing signs of being in love. This she had sensed now for some days; she had wondered about it; worried about it; and now felt sure of it and had no intention that such things should proceed along their natural course.

"Elizabeth . . . tell me, dearest, why would you not see Mr. Clay?"

Elizabeth studied her own toe with interest. "I . . . I

did not wish to. I am tired from shopping . . ." she offered lamely.

"Nonsense! You are not and never have been prone to a delicate turn! No, my pet, that does not fit."

"But truly, mother . . . 'tis nothing more . . ." tried Elizabeth, intent now on the floral pattern of her bedside rug.

"I see. Then there is nothing wrong?"

"No . . . I only wanted a bit of rest. I don't mean to be rude, mother . . ."

"Then don't be, my dear," interrupted her mother, reproaching her gently.

Elizabeth bit her lip and waited for the inevitable as her mother continued. "I am not in my dotage, child. There are some things I can see, and what I see is not to my liking. You and Mr. Clay have found each other . . . charming. It is not surprising however, a rift has occurred— I care not what caused it, for it is just as well. I take leave to advise you, my love, that I would never countenance a match between you and Mr. Clay!"

"I . . . I don't know what you mean," said Elizabeth, not meeting her mama's eye.

"Don't you? Very well, have it your way as long as you know the way of it. Really though, Elizabeth, how you can have thought of Mr. Clay . . . why he is just a common gamester!"

"Oh, that is really quite bad of you, mama!" Elizabeth was moved to express. "His name is amongst the oldest on Wight . . . his connections are quite high . . . and . . ."

Her mother put up a hand to halt this flow. "There is no question as to the gentility of his birth. However, he has set aside that quality by buying and running a gaming hell!

When he did that, he took himself out of the world of *ton*. Why must you and Jewelene think him some sort of hero?"

"But he is, mama! He lost his arm in an act of bravery, as well you know, in fact, have often said you admired. He runs a gaming hell because his father died in debt, and he sacrificed himself in order to give his mother and sister the things they had grown used to!" Again, she bit her lip and looked away. What did it matter? Why was she defending him?

"Now understand me, child, I will not have you courted by such as he! Do you think I want to see my daughter the wife of a *casino owner?* You and Jewelene have been a sore trial to me. Shall I never see either one of you comfortably settled? Shall I never cease having to worry myself over your futures?"

"Oh, please mother . . ." cried Elizabeth, dissolving in tears.

Mrs. Debb caught a sob in her throat. Elizabeth, her poor sweet Elizabeth, was really suffering and she was most attached to her daughter. She went to her at once and put an arm about her shoulders, rocking her gently and soothingly. "There, there, don't fret, love . . . everything will work out."

"No, no, it never shall. You say his courting nay . . . and I must obey from filial duty as well as my own inclination. I would not marry Ben Clay were he the only man left standing on this earth!"

Mrs. Debbs did not find this piece of news as gratifying as one might assume—indeed, quite the reverse.

Eighteen

Jewelene and the marquess had watched Lightning do both the half-mile and the mile run. His timing was better than she could have hoped for; however, the marquess stood frowning for a long while after his first exclamation of "Bravo!"

"What is it?" asked the lady who thought more than bravo was in order.

"Eh? Naught, child . . . look, Jewelene, where did James say he was going?"

"Portsmouth . . . to raise the money for the fee at Derby . . . and then home. Why?"

They were already walking back to the house, but he stopped, "You go on, I have something to speak to Jonas about."

She gazed at him for a long moment, "To Jonas? But . . ."

He touched her cheek with his finger. "Don't fratch over it, love, 'tis naught but a whim."

She blushed. "I am certain I would not trouble myself over anything *you* chose to do." She was already walking away from him.

"Till later, love . . . for I won't be in for dinner." And then grinned to himself at her quick turnabout.

"You won't?" she said, betraying some disappointment in spite of herself. However, she made a quick recovery. "Well then, 'tis good day to you, sir, for I shall be retiring early."

"Will you, love? Odd, for even yet I have hopes of

meeting you again tonight." It was softly spoken, a hint underlining the words.

She stared at him a moment, then frowned in puzzlement. What could he mean? Surely he was but dallying in some odd manner of his own . . . for he couldn't know she was Babette. He just couldn't. She shrugged off such a horrendous notion and gave him her back, making swiftly for the house. He watched her long, deeply amused.

He then turned and stalked Jonas, a small angular man of some forty years.

"Jonas, I would have word with you."

"Would ye, sir? Aboot what, sir?"

"First, I know that young James means to enter Lightning. Does it not seem odd to you that he should be gone a week, return, then off again to Derby?"

"I don't reetly remember discussing the way of it with Sir James," said Jonas cautiously.

"Trust me, Jonas, I mean to aid Sir James and his sister if I can, but there are some things I must know."

Jonas studied him a moment. "Aye . . . but there be some that thinks ye ain't pound dealing with m'mistress and Sir James."

"Oh?" said the marquess eyeing him for a moment.

"Before I was groom for Sir James . . . I was sech for his father. Went to London with him and his lady more often than not. The Marquess of Lyndhurst . . . he be a notable figure aboot town, happen, he was pointed out on occasion . . . ye catch m'drift . . . m'lord?"

The marquess was taken aback. "You know? Yet . . . you haven't given me away . . . why?"

"Happen . . . I thought it for the best at the time . . . happen it might turn out reet well . . . but as to giving over on Sir James without his leave . . ." he scratched his chin, "now . . . that be a different matter."

"All right then . . . bear with me while I think aloud, and do feel free to stop me if you believe my . . . fancy unequal to reality." He gazed at the groom, his observant eyes noting the light in the older man's dark eyes. "Let us assume," he continued, "that young James and his friend have been successful. They have in Portsmouth obtained the necessary blunt to enter Lightning for the Derby race. Ah, now would two such young fellows return home before they have gone to Derby and seen the thing through?" He shook his head. "No, Sir James is of a different stamp . . . he would have gone straight to Derby. Now, let us see . . . the trip for two energetic young men would take six days there and back. So we should see him very shortly for he must return and take Lightning on the journey to Derby." He eyed the groom again. "It would appear that thus far, I have not erred, but Jonas, you and Sir James have."

"I don't see the fit . . . meaning no disrespect, m'lord."

"Don't you? Lightning here is the sole collateral behind Sir James's investment. If anything were to happen to this horse . . ."

"Aye, but what should be happening to him?"

"That is precisely why I chose to speak to you. Why is Lightning stabled out here, so far away from the house . . . away from the stables?"

" 'Tis the season, m'lord . . . he be getting his blood up every time he sniff a mare, and the stables . . . well, they house a filly or two bound to drive the poor fellow into fratching and champing . . ."

"And who stands guard over him at night, Jonas?"

"Wot now? I don't get your drift, m'lord . . . there be nobbut m'self, and I sleep in the hayloft above more than not . . ." He stopped and gave a low whistle, "Gawks, m'lord . . . be ye thinking there's mischief afoot?"

"It seems to me that Lightning is a valuable prize, Jonas, and where there is value, there is trouble."

"Lordy . . . but wot ye got in mind?"

"Did I say I had anything in mind, Jonas?" he grinned at the older man's expression. "However, as it happens, I do have a thought or two, and . . ."

Jewelene sat down to dinner with Lyla and her Aunt Dora. They had but a moment to wait on Elizabeth, who made a tardy appearance and that only at her mother's insistence. Elizabeth's mood was despondent and added little to the strained hour. Robby was not present to alleviate Lyla's frustration, and strangely, restlessly, Jewelene felt Keith's absence. 'Twas a fact and one that bothered her more than she cared to admit to herself.

"Are you sure the marquess said he would not be in to dinner tonight?" asked Lyla of Mrs. Debbs, hoping yet for Robby's appearance.

"Quite, dear. In fact, he said he was dining out with friends and would not be in until a very late hour. But my, we are a dull group without the men. I was hoping the marquess's very charming cousin would have been here . . . but Jewelene tells me he too has made other plans."

Lyla turned to Elizabeth and eyed her curiously, "Whyever are you so sour, Liz dear? I can't imagine why you would not see Ben . . . he left in a vile temper this afternoon."

"I am sure I don't know why," said Elizabeth turning her cheek away.

"Oh?" said Lyla, again eyeing her but this time with something of a dawning light, "But . . . how very droll . . . you are upset by what Omsbury told us! My word! I didn't realize 'twas that way with you. When Ben insisted we dash madly back here, I thought it was because he didn't want you telling Jewelene about that French creature of his . . . but . . ."

However, she did not get to complete her sentence for Elizabeth made a choking sound, threw her napkin onto the table, and charged from the room. This, all beneath the startled eyes of the servants and the frown of her mother.

Mrs. Debbs eyed the servants before turning a repressing glance on Lyla. "Really dear . . . such talk at the dinner table!"

Lyla blushed, but it was obvious to Jewelene that the girl was bursting with her discovery. Thus, it was a strained meal. Jewelene believed she understood, still, she wanted to escape the table and confirm her suspicions. It was with relief that she saw the meal at its end and desultory conversation put aside. With quick wit she put out her hand and detained Lyla from following her aunt. "Oh, there is a tear in your hem, love," said Jewelene. "Come with me and I shall repair the thing in a trice."

"But, but . . . I don't see . . ." started Lyla.

" 'Tis in the back, dear, how could you see?" rejoined Jewelene, bearing Lyla off.

Once inside her room with the door bolted, she turned on the pert brunette. "Now, little girl, what did Omsbury tell you and Elizabeth today?"

"Oh dear . . . I don't know that Ben will approve of my repeating . . ."

Jewelene advanced menacingly. "Give over, brat—now!"

"Oh, very well, and I must say, Jewelene, there is no need to hurl names at me." Then observing the dangerous look cast her way she repeated quickly what Omsbury had said, topping it with ". . . and imagine Ben taking up with a *Frenchwoman* . . . she must be very vulgar too . . . and I must say I never thought it of him. How could I when *he* is forever preaching the proprieties to me . . ."

"Do shut up, Lyla, I must think!"

"Oh, now I daresay I've thrown you into the dismals over it . . . at least you have more right . . . after all, you've been hanging on Ben's sleeve these two . . ."

"If you don't shut up all by your little self, I shall gag you, tie you, and feed you to the sea!" threatened Jewelene. "Hang on his sleeve indeed! Ben and I have never been more than good friends . . . a sister is what I have been . . . more so than you! Your brother is in trouble now because of a cad and you can do naught but wag your tongue! I must think! Dear God, was there ever such a tangle?"

"I don't know what you are talking about," snapped Lyla "and, besides, what can *I* do? 'Tis he that has chosen this wench . . . and why should I do aught to interfere?"

"Why indeed? Do go away, Lyla."

Lyla rose in an indignant huff and left Jewelene to her thoughts.

It had come to this, she was at *point non plus!* Elizabeth would have to be taken into her confidence. There was no other way to convince her that Ben was not having an affair with another woman, but it was not a good thing. Elizabeth was bound to be shocked, and there was no saying what Elizabeth might do when she was shocked!

Jewelene played with her long curls and sighed. Nothing to do but get it over, for she was not about to allow Elizabeth to torture herself needlessly.

She made her way down the wide hall and stopped before her cousin's door. She knocked gently at first but when she found she was not answered, she tried the knob and found the door unbolted. Slowly she stuck in her head and saw Elizabeth stretched out across her mauve-colored bed. Jewelene went in, closing the door behind her.

"Lizzie?"

"Oh . . . Jewelene . . ." started Elizabeth.

"Your fire is dying out," said Jewelene, going to the hearth and placing a log in the grate. She smacked her hands together dusting off the dirt. "There . . . oh, just look at those stars . . ." she said, going to the window.

Elizabeth watched her, frowning. What was this cousin of hers up to? She loved Jewelene and believed she knew her well. She was leading up to something, she could just feel it.

"Jewel?"

"Indeed, you mean to tell me not to go tonight!" she clasped her hands together. "I knew you had guessed! The moment Lyla told me that Omsbury had spoken of Ben's connection to Babette . . . I knew, just knew you had guessed the whole!" This on a tragic note.

"But Jewel . . ." began Elizabeth, sitting up fully, eyes wide.

"No, I must go, darling. 'Tis the only way. We cannot be certain that Jimmy will get enough cash to enter Lightning . . . so you see, I must play my part again."

"Your part? Go? Jewelene . . . I have never thought myself without understanding but . . ."

"You are going to say how risky it is. But indeed, love, with my black wig and French accent . . . and outrageous gowns . . ."

"French accent?" picked up Elizabeth at once.

"Yes, to hear me you would never guess that I have never been to France!"

Elizabeth gasped, "You . . . you are the Frenchwoman Omsbury spoke of?"

"Oh, good gracious! Then you did not know! Oh, how dreadful, I have given myself away without need. I thought it certain you knew . . . for how could you believe a man like Ben Clay would play you false?"

Elizabeth made a strange sound and threw her arms about her cousin. "Lud, Jewel, will you never cease to amaze me? But how is this? Tell me at once, you wretched girl!"

And so Jewelene gave it to her from the beginning and, when her tale was at an end, her cousin sighed, "Oh, but Jewel . . . it worries me."

"Does it? Why?"

"It's the marquess's cousin. There is something about him . . . he is so much more knowing than he would have us believe. It seems odd that he would hound you as Babette and not see Babette in Jewelene!"

"You are wrong. The marquess's handsome cousin is naught but a rakehell. He chases a woman for the sport . . . seeing little but the color of her hair and the turn of her ankle!" There was a tinge of bitterness in Jewelene's tone, and Elizabeth cast her a quick look.

"Don't go tonight, Jewelene. After all you have said . . .

I am fearful . . . fearful of Omsbury should he see you too often. There is no saying but that he might find a similarity and then . . . good Lord . . ."

So, Jewelene had not gone. She retired to her room quite early in the evening. Her thoughts did battle within. She was at war and she was not quite certain of the enemy. Was it her heart? Was it her will . . . or was it the ginger-haired devil-man plaguing her fancy? Now, sitting in her room, wishing she were at the Silver Heart playing Babette, hearing his voice in her ear, thrilling to his touch, she wondered at herself. Oh, oh Jewelene, you are on dangerous turf now, m'girl. Such as he would break your virgin heart.

At the Silver Heart the marquess stood in the main gaming room watching the play at the faro table. Where was she? Had something gone amiss? Had she sustained a fall riding across the fields? It was all too possible . . .

He found Ben Clay. "Where the devil is she?"

"I don't know. Perhaps she could not get away tonight," said Ben frowning.

"Perhaps," agreed the marquess thoughtfully.

Ben stared at him a long moment. "There is nothing we can do but wait."

"Is there not?" said the marquess quietly. "You will excuse me if I forego the pleasure of your tables tonight, sir," with which he was gone.

Some twenty minutes later he was taking the stairs two at a time and stopping at Jewelene's door. His knock was soft enough, its answering response softer, yet it had the power to revive his harried spirits.

Jewelene sat straight up in her bed and looked at the man filling the doorway. It did strange things to her, the sight of him.

"You are all right then?" he said softly.

"Of course . . . why should I not be?" asked Jewelene, much surprised.

"My mistake, Jewelene . . . do forgive me."

She inclined her head dismissing him, but before he could close the door to her room she called out, "Did you not do well at the Silver Heart tonight?"

"I did not play."

"Oh . . . but how odd. Why then did you go?"

"Why? An excellent question. I had some whim at the start of the evening. It waned when I discovered the one thing I desired at the Silver Heart was not to be found there tonight. Good night, child."

"Good night . . . and *I am not a child!*" she snapped, plumping her head down on her pillow and giving him her back.

He closed her door, chuckling lightly to himself. So, she had decided to remain at home tonight. There was no telling what Jewelene would do next. No telling at all.

Nineteen

The following four bittersweet days went by swiftly for Jewelene. She was torn by the conflicting emotions Keith aroused in her breast. She was torn by her own perverseness. After that first absence, Babette returned to the faro table, and Keith was ever by her side at night, saucily flirting with her. By daylight she walked, rode, and talked with him, drawn to him in a way she had never experienced with anyone else.

How could he? It was a constant question, ever present, ever playing havoc with all her better senses. How could he make such bold, cavalier love to her by night, when she was Babette, and yet tease, flirt, and attempt to win her heart by day, when she was herself? Only a hardened rake, an unfeeling knave would do such a thing. And she could not help but feel that this handsome ginger-haired man was not the womanizer his actions would lead one to believe.

The marquess was enjoying the game, it was nearing its end, and he had in mind something of a finale. But first he wanted Jewelene to accept his proposal without knowing he was the Marquess of Lyndhurst. This was something he would have to work out. He would have to tell her he knew that she and Babette were one and the same. The thought of her expression when such information was released sent him into a round of indecent mirth. Yes, he would enjoy that. And then, then he would tell her she was to be his wife. Or rather, he would ask her and, Lord, did he look forward to hearing her answer. More then anything he wanted to hear Jewelene say "yes" to Keith Robendale, a second son of little prospect . . . a penniless gamester. Ah . . . "yes" and then . . .

Was that not romance at its height . . . as the gods intended? Was it not such to set a man, even a worldly-wise fellow like himself, to dreaming?

Oblivious to all this were Sir James and his friend. They had traveled to Derby and back, and the Henshaw grounds lay in sight.

"Egad, but 'tis good to be home!" ejaculated Sir James, coming out of deep thought. "Don't mind telling you, Art, been worrying m'self ever since I clapped eyes on Omsbury's man."

"Aye, thought as much . . . though why has me fairly chaffed," said Arthur.

"Hang it, Art! Thought you would have realized. Left Lightning with Jonas, you know. Now, mind, Jonas is the best of good grooms . . . loyal as a hound, but, he don't expect any mischief. . . ."

"Mischief?" interrupted Arthur, "what sort?"

" 'Tis this. Omsbury wants m'sister. Don't see why . . . I mean, he is old enough to be her father, and she more than most could handle. But that don't signify. What does is the fact that Lightning . . . in a manner of speaking, stands between Omsbury and Jewelene's hand."

Arthur shook his head, "Don't see that! Why it stands to reason . . . that ain't a horse's job . . . fact is, rather think *you* stand between his lordship and Jewelene."

Sir James stopped his horse and cast a look of total disdain over his long-time friend. "Dolt! Nodcock! Your brains are addled! Don't you see at all?"

"Well, as to that . . . I rather thought I did . . ." said Arthur, puzzling over this last.

"Noddy! You've got maggots in your upper works! Now listen to me. We have got to do something to guard Lightning from abduction."

"Who would want to steal Lightning?" said Arthur unwisely.

"May the saints give me patience!" Sir James rolled his eyes heavenward. "Omsbury would want to steal him."

"Don't see that. It don't fit for one thing . . . know for a fact his pockets are plump . . . rich as a nabob . . ."

"Daft. Not for the money! For Jewelene! Don't you dare interrupt me . . ." he warned, seeing that Arthur was about to do just that.

"Now listen carefully. He knows we Henshaws have poured our last penny into the estate. He knows Jewelene has an affection for me . . . has notions of my setting off for Cambridge as our father did at my age. He knows then that we pin a great deal of hope on Lightning to pull in enough to allow us to get by . . . and he waits on Jewelene's answer. She knows *I* don't want the match . . . I know *she* don't want it . . . but she puts him off . . . till the race . . . do you understand now?"

"Not quite."

He was eyed with a great deal of exasperation. "Don't you? By all that is holy, how could you not?"

"She won't marry him . . . not even to send you to Cambridge . . . she is not the sort to give in so easily," said Arthur somewhat irritably. "If you don't know her well enough to know that, then 'tis you that are the dolt . . . not I."

Sir James frowned. "That may have been true. But,

Art . . . it came to me at Derby, thinking about Omsbury's man. I've put Jewelene on a precarious road. I've taken a loan from a moneylender at an exorbitant rate of interest. If anything *were* to happen to Lightning now . . . good Lord! She'd not blink over marrying Omsbury . . . she'd believe she had no choice."

Arthur frowned and as this rang true he shook his head sadly.

"Aye . . . now you've done it!"

Omsbury sat in his library, his eyes narrowed over what he had just learned. He sipped his sherry and got to his feet. "So, they have that damnable horse safely hidden away, do they? Think they've outwitted me, no doubt! Well . . . well . . . Miss Henshaw, my pretty needle-witted bird, I'm not in the least put out." He turned to Jenkins who stood about shuffling his feet.

"Jenkins, you will discover when it is Sir James means to travel with Lightning to Derby and then, my man . . ."

Jewelene sat in her room, brooding—'twas a new pastime she had acquired. It was nearly teatime and that very fact served to make her restless. *He,* that dashing, ginger-haired devil, had gone out earlier, saying flippantly that he would return to have tea with her. She had retorted that he needn't bother, but he had laughed and called over his shoulder that it was no bother at all. Oh! That had made her furious! He was insufferable! And here she was counting the moments till his return, dressing for his eyes, for the light in his eyes that had the power to warm her blood! Oh! She loathed him and herself as well.

A knock at her door and she turned from her reflection

in the looking glass and answered in a tone that spelled her preoccupation, "Yes?"

" 'Tis me, Wilma, with the jewel box you wanted," said a timid voice on the other side of the door.

"Oh, come in, Wilma," said Jewelene, smiling to herself. She had donned a gown of rich gold, nearly the shade of her hair, and she wanted the topaz pendant and matching earrings to accent the gown.

Wilma did not look at ease, a circumstance that did not go unnoticed by Jewelene. She remarked upon it. "Whatever has you in such a fidget, dear . . . you couldn't possibly be frightened of *me*?"

"Oh, no, Miss Jewelene . . . 'tis that pleased I am to be serving ye, but, but . . ."

"But what, girl?" asked Jewelene, much surprised.

"Could I not just give ye the topaz set . . . must ye need the whole box?"

Jewelene's brows went up. What was this? What sort of thing was Wilma proposing and why? "Wilma . . . why do you not want me to see my own jewel case? Whatever is wrong?"

"Oh, Lordy, miss . . . 'tis but what I promised Sir James. He said . . . jest give Miss Jewelene whatever she asks for out of the box, but on no account was I to give ye the entire box . . . and . . . meaning no disrespect . . . who am I to answer to?"

Jewelene was astonished. "Leave the box with me, Wilma, and then run off. You shall not have to answer to Sir James, for he would not expect you to disobey my orders!" Her tone was firm but not unkind.

"Yes, miss," said the girl, rushing to make her escape.

Jewelene saw the door close, and then her eyes went to

the large jewel case. It was a wooden box intricately carved and well polished. What had Jimmy been up to? Her heart beat uncomfortably, for already she felt the first tingling of fear. She opened the lid, knowing before her hand took out the layers of wood that her mother's diamond set would not be there. She closed her eyes, an empty feeling in her stomach. Sold them? No, Jimmy would never do that, they were a family heirloom, and she was not so naive. He had used them to obtain a loan! Oh God, Jimmy!

She felt as though her mind could not bear this new burden. She had rarely lost her temper with her brother. He was her pet, her darling, she adored him, and wanted him always to love her, but if her suspicions were true . . .

Her head tilted as she heard the sudden commotion that inevitably occurs with a new arrival. Keith . . . that Keith had returned was her first thought, and she dashed out, forgetting to don the topaz set. She brought herself up short at the balcony overlooking the hall when she saw the arrival was not Keith at all, but her brother.

"Jimmy!" she screeched taking the stairs much like a charging filly.

"Whoa there, Jewel . . . don't bowl me over!" laughed her brother.

She flung her arms about him, for here he was, home safe and perhaps, with any luck, her suspicions might prove false. Over his shoulder she gave Arthur a sunny smile of welcome and then, taking up her brother's hand, she said quickly, "Come, let's go into the parlor for tea. Aunt is visiting with Lady Stanway, and Lyla and Elizabeth are out riding with Robby." She tugged at his hand

and led both young men into the parlor, carefully closing the door after them.

"I . . ." she started, not taking a seat, forcing them to remain standing, "am not going to ask how you fared, I can see for myself that you are both quite well. I am not going to ask Art to leave us alone, Jimmy . . . because . . . he probably knows more than I. Therefore, without hemming . . . without giving me a round tale, did you take mama's diamonds . . . the family diamonds . . . did you, Jimmy?"

Sir James looked taken aback. He then swept his hand through his light brown curls and complained, "Servants! Can't be trusted. Told that girl she wasn't to give you the case!"

"For pity's sake!" balked his sister. "Did you think any servant could refuse me my own jewel case? And that is not the point! What have you done, Jimmy . . . what?"

"I've entered Lightning . . . naught else matters!"

"You've . . . you've already been to Derby?"

"Aye . . . and shall be off again in two days with our horse. Want to travel slow with him. But he is entered and . . ."

"And what if we lose? Have you thought of that? Oh, Jimmy, how could you do anything so, so . . . ramshackled? If we lose . . . there go the Henshaw diamonds . . . and what will the trustees say?"

"Aye, and there's the interest on the loan . . ." put in Arthur, shaking his head. "That's the thing . . . *can't* lose! Actually, *mustn't* . . ."

They eyed one another with considerable agitation and some misgiving. And then Jewelene heard a voice that made her want to cry out and run into big strong arms.

"Hello, Sir James!" greeted Keith, coming into the room. As he shook hands with Jimmy, he nodded at Arthur, "Salford. How was your little trip? No trouble, I presume?"

"Good to see you, Robendale. No, no trouble . . . discounting . . ." said Arthur, not catching Jimmy's eye, "the fact that Omsbury's groom took to trailing us . . ."

"What?" shrieked Jewelene. She was still standing, but upon hearing this, she sank into a near-by cushioned chair.

The marquess stood beside her. His hand reached out and took hers. He had reached the parlor door in time to hear enough to know that Sir James had gone to a moneylender. Things were serious indeed, and as he scanned Jewelene's face and saw that she was deeply agitated, he knew that the game was at an end. He would not allow her to suffer any longer.

"Never mind, Jewelene. Omsbury will do us no harm," he said reassuringly.

She looked up at him. He sounded so confident, but what did it matter to him? It wasn't his problem. She turned to Jimmy.

"But Jimmy, why would Omsbury's groom follow you to Derby?"

"He didn't . . . though I have a strong suspicion he knew whither we were bound."

"Did he . . ." she stopped and looked hesitantly at Keith, "could Omsbury's man . . . have guessed . . . what you went to Portsmouth . . . to do?"

"I am afraid so, sis," James replied gravely.

"It doesn't matter," said Keith, raising her hand to his lips. "I promise you that. Can you trust me, love?"

"I . . . I want to."

"Then do so," he said quietly. "Trust your instincts, Jewelene."

More than this he could not say now and was spared her questions by the parlor doors flying open to admit Lyla Clay, Elizabeth, Robby, and Lord Omsbury.

Twenty

"Jewelene . . . only do look and see who is coming to join us for tea!" cried Lyla jubilantly as she whipped off her riding hat of brown velvet and dropped it onto a nearby stool. Then spying Sir James lounging against the corner of the fireplace, she put out her hands to him, "Why . . . James . . . how wonderful to have you home!"

He dropped a dutiful kiss upon her outstretched hand, and his eyes twinkled as they met hers. She was a saucy wench, this Lyla, and she attracted him no little bit, but he had no intention of getting caught up in her wiles. "Hello, Lyla! *Certes*, but you make a man wish he had never left!"

She smiled mischievously at him. "Indeed . . . you naughty boy! But lud, James, we have been quite dull without you . . . and Arthur there." She bade Art welcome with her large eyes. "Haven't we, Jewelene?" she called out gaily, feeling much in spirits. She had been out riding with a marquess and a baron, and since Ben had also arrived on the scene, quite occupying Elizabeth's time, she had been able to impress both gentlemen with her many charms. Lud, but she was in heaven.

Jewelene heard her but found it difficult to respond to the chit's enthusiasm, for Lord Omsbury was bending over her hand, lingering and looking full into her green eyes. "I have missed you, Jewelene. Faith, love, I did not realize how much . . . until this very moment!"

She had to admit he was an accomplished flirt at any

rate, and there was that in his eyes that made her feel . . . almost sorry for him. He had chosen her. He believed himself in love and he was being rejected. For someone like him . . . it must be very hard.

Yet, she found Omsbury's intensity almost humiliating under Keith's penetrating scrutiny. She was forced to play the lamb, and it was a difficult role to essay. "You are . . . too kind, my lord," was all she could of think to answer.

Keith's upper lip had worked itself into a sneer. Robby was at his side. "Tried not to bring him along, Keith . . . but there was nothing for it when Lyla insisted. Elizabeth didn't like it much, either . . . but there you are. Sorry."

"Never mind, Rob, I'll handle it," answered the marquess.

"Jewelene . . . I am sure no one will object if we continue with our plans." He turned to Sir James, "Your sister and I were going to take a walk to the hothouse and skip tea."

"Excellent notion!" said Jimmy at once, aware that Jewelene wanted to escape Omsbury.

Lyla was all too wary of Jewelene's power over Omsbury, a man she had quite made up her mind to have— over Sir James and even over Robby.

She therefore added her approval. "Indeed, Mr. Robendale . . . there are some marvelous gardenia plants now blooming. The aroma is enchanting."

Omsbury turned aside to Keith. "Very neatly executed, Mr. Robendale."

"I rather thought so, Omsbury," said Keith smiling grimly. He offered his arm to Jewelene. She took it, rose to her feet, and bade them all a pleasant tea.

In the hall she turned to Keith and squeezed his arm, "Thank you . . . so much. I will just run up and fetch my spencer."

"I will await you outdoors," he said, and his smile caressed her.

He watched her take the stairs, smiling after her for a moment before his brows drew together. He was far more bothered by this latest turn of events than he would allow her to realize. Sir James had done a very foolish thing, and Omsbury was a dangerous enemy. It was evident Omsbury meant to have Jewelene, and he would have to tread carefully and be more than usually watchful if Jewelene weren't to be thrown into a situation from which she would not be able to extricate herself.

He paced outdoors, his hat tilted over his left eye, gloved hands clasped at his back. She came upon him, and her smile was warm, "Goodness! You look . . . bothered. What is it?"

"Naught, child . . ." he started.

She took umbrage at once, she would not have it. Every time he was with her alone, he called her "child." She disliked it intensely, especially when she recalled that he never once called Babette "child"! "I am not a child, and don't try to spare me. If you don't wish to confide in me, 'tis one matter. But do not behave as though I am not mature enough to understand!"

"Was I doing that?" he asked, surprised. "I hadn't thought so."

"Well, you were . . . you do it all the time!" she snapped.

"I shall take care never to do it in the future. Am I forgiven?" he asked contritely, smiling down at her lovely profile.

She relented. "It would be quite ungrateful of me not to forgive you when you have just rescued me from the dragon."

"Ah, I take it Omsbury is the dragon," he said.

She sighed, " 'Tis cruel of me, I suppose . . . but I cannot like him."

"Cruel of you? How so?" he asked, much taken aback by this outlook.

"Why . . . the man does pay me court . . . and I have not totally rejected him, have I? I mean . . . not really. It leads him on, I suppose . . . and even if it did not, 'tis cruel to reject anyone. But all the same, I do not like him," again she sighed.

He eyed her a moment, halting his steps, and she looked round and found his gaze tenderly upon her. "You are a wonder, Jewelene."

She laughed uneasily and then brought up a matter she had meant to broach to him. "Jonas tells me you and he have found a place to shelter Lightning at night . . . some place out of the way?"

"Yes, I hope you don't mind. I thought it . . . best," he said, looking straight ahead.

"No, indeed. Under the circumstances I think it an excellent notion. Thank you."

"Not yet, Jewelene. Don't thank me yet. I shall ask for payment in due time . . . in due time, and then I shall want far more than gratitude," he said looking at her, a twinkle calling forth one of her own.

It was these last words she recalled as she raised her eyes from the faro dealing box and saw him standing there. It was a moment indeed . . . all else faded out. The marquess made his way unobtrusively, deftly, to her side. And then her ungloved hand was in his, and his lips cherished the feel of her flesh, and his eyes made bold love to her.

"Babette . . ." he said softly, "the day has been overlong!"

She felt herself ruffle in spite of the heat he inspired. Oooh, what a cad! How the very duplicity of his words enraged her! Really, it was the outside of enough! However, she managed to rein in her temper.

"Has it, *mon cher? Hein?* The little Henshaw . . . she does not amuse you?" teased Babette, her eyes glittering through the holes in her black mask.

"She amuses me much . . . almost as much as you, but let us not speak of her, when we can speak of *us.*"

"But me . . . I do not say we may speak of us . . . and please do not kiss my shoulder . . ."

"That's right, Keith! Take yourself bloody well away!" said Filey who stood at her other side.

The marquess ignored him. However, he did cease a moment later for another man had entered the gaming room, a man whom the marquess would not have eyeing this table—or Babette.

"Excuse me, my love," the marquess apologized.

She sent him a quick doubtful look and then saw the object of his intent. *"Mais oui . . ."* she said, wondering what he was about.

The marquess drew himself up before Lord Omsbury, matching him sneer for sneer. Omsbury employed affectations, and did so now by bringing up his quizzing glass. "Oh, 'tis you, Robendale."

"Indeed, your sight has not failed you, my lord," said Keith blandly, "nor your memory—one hears such tales of the maladies accompanying . . . *age.*" A flush hit!

Omsbury grew red-cheeked, but he still maintained his cool exterior. "You did not approach me to exchange quips, Robendale, therefore one wonders what has brought you hither?"

"My weariness. 'Tis a sad thing indeed. I have been here more than a week and yet have not yet found a worthy opponent to engage in *écarté*!"

"Ah, allow me to offer you my sympathy, sir," said Omsbury mockingly.

"I would rather you offered to be my adversary," the marquess continued. "One hears of your prowess at the game and one is . . . intrigued."

"Indeed? But I rather fancy you have not . . . what it takes to play a game with me."

"Perhaps, my lord, you have underestimated your man," retorted the marquess, his eyes challenging.

Omsbury regarded him a long moment before saying slowly, "You surprise me, sir. However, do let us play. You may name the stakes."

The marquess inclined his head. "I am too much a gamester, my lord, to both challenge and name the stakes!"

"Very well, shall we say 500 pounds a set, 1000 per vole."

Nary a muscle flinched in the marquess's lean body. "Indeed, I find such stakes most . . . er . . . stimulating," he answered.

"Really? I had not realized you were so affluent, in fact, I had reason to believe quite the opposite."

"Did you? How odd!" said the marquess. "But, my lord, we digress. The game has been decided, the stakes have been named, it needs only the time."

Omsbury studied his timepiece. "Shall we say in an hour? I had intended to try my luck at the E.O. table."

The marquess again inclined his head, this time in acquiescence. "Then 11 it is, my lord. I look forward to it."

Omsbury moved away and the marquess too turned his back. He saw Jewelene watching him, a fearful look in her eyes. He wanted to be alone with her but knew if he were to go up to her and ask her to walk with him, she would not. He chuckled over this, for she had such a contrary nature. However, she was itching with curiosity. There left but one thing to do—saunter away.

He had little doubt that she would follow, and follow Jewelene did. She caught up to him just before he reached the stairs.

"Mon cher . . . you are leaving?" she asked, much surprised.

"Of course not. Did it frighten you, love, to think I was?"

She put up her chin. "Frighten? Don't be nonsensical."

He had come forward, he was standing over her, his eyes caressing her. How dare he, she kept thinking; she wished with all her heart she could rip off her mask and expose his duplicity. But she could not, and part of her wanted him to talk so, to look so . . .

"What . . . what did zat dreadful man want of you?" she asked breathlessly.

"Omsbury? He wanted none of me. 'Twas I that wanted to have at him."

"Why?" she asked, feeling she had no air left to her.

"Come with me and I shall tell you," he said, leading her down the hall again to Ben's private office. He took her in, closed the door at his back.

She eyed him, a brow raised. "Well then . . . speak."

He bowed mockingly but his eyes twinkled, "As you command me, love. You asked me why I should want to have at Omsbury. And thus I shall tell you. He angers me with his forced attentions upon one who is very dear to me."

"Oh? Who eez thees person?"

He was too close to her, she thought she would suffocate, but she could do naught to stop him as his arms went round her. "I thought you knew, darling. 'Tis the woman I would wive . . . 'tis my only love . . . Jewelene!"

She gasped, but it was short-lived for his mouth already covered hers. When she was able to pull away, "You . . . you . . . know?"

"Almost from the start," he chuckled.

"You . . . you have used me . . . abominably!" she accused.

"I could not resist it . . . or you . . ." His eyes adored and she blushed beneath his gaze.

"You . . . you are a wretch!" she called down upon him.

"No doubt you are right," he agreed amiably.

She stopped, her brows drawn together, and then she said almost on a pout, "Earlier tonight . . . you said . . . you cared more for Babette."

He laughed aloud. "I thought that would chaff. I said I was *amused* more by Babette . . . and you must admit, naughty love, you are far more devilish with your mask on than off!"

The door opened, and Ben appeared. He looked from one to the other and grinned, "I came because I thought you might need me, puss, but I stand corrected!"

"No, you have arrived in time. Help me convince Babette here to go home . . . *now*," said the marquess.

"Indeed, I agree with you. What if Jimmy comes in?" suggested Ben.

"No, I won't go . . . we have a deal, Ben," said she, stamping her foot.

" 'Tis ended then," said Ben grinning broadly.

"I won't leave. Keith has challenged Omsbury to a game. I mean to see it," said she.

Ben raised a brow, "Have you? What . . . piquet?"

"No, écarté."

"Devil you say! He is unbeatable at it," thundered Ben.

"Perhaps," was all the marquess answered. He then turned to Jewelene, his eyes caressed her, his lips kissed her hand. "Until later, love. We have much to talk about." Then to Ben, "See to it that she doesn't get into any trouble."

"Ha!" answered the woman of the marquess's heart, "I shall get into as much trouble as I like!"

Twenty-one

The marquess met his cousin as he sauntered down the hall.

"Why, Robby . . . come to look in on me? You've chosen an opportune time."

"Have I? Why, what's toward?" asked his plump cousin warily.

"Challenged Omsbury to écarté. . . . 500 a trick, 1000 a vole!"

"*Certes!* Mean you to put him under the table? No one can beat you at écarté. In fact . . . don't know anyone who would take you on. How came he to do so?"

"Thinks himself rather a top sawyer of a player . . . but then, he doesn't realize he is playing the Marquess of Lyndhurst, now does he?"

"Which brings me to it. Been thinking about it. You've been playing a deep game, Keith, and what's more . . . don't like it this time—not that I ever do—but this time 'tis different. I mean . . . the Henshaw chit . . . 'tis time you own up the wager is fairly mine!"

"So it is," laughed the marquess.

"Then . . . do you mean to tell her?" asked Robby hopefully.

"I do—tonight in fact. Right after this game."

"Thank God for that! I don't mind telling you . . . haven't liked being you!" said Robby.

His cousin laughed and put an arm through his cousin's as he scanned the room for Omsbury. Finding him, he signaled the hour, and his lordship came forth.

They left the E.O. chamber, again going into the long hall, traversing its width to yet another card room. Here a lackey was sent after the two écarté packs before they took up their seats facing one another.

A murmur went round the room, and several men standing in small groups made a path their way. Casino écarté was a two-handed game, but it allowed spectator betting which often made it tense and most exciting.

Two fresh decks were brought for the players' inspection. They would be alternated during the deals, for écarté only used thirty-two cards. Omsbury drew and received a ten of spades, the marquess the nine of hearts. The deal went to the high card and Omsbury scooped the deck into his hand smugly, already cocksure.

The eleventh card was turned over as a trump and when it showed a king, a low whistle went round the table.

"Your point, Omsbury. It would indeed seem that you are lucky," said the marquess, not in the least perturbed.

By the time several hands were played, they had drawn quite a crowd, and the betting was already with Omsbury. However, Ben had been quietly watching both players and, as the last hand of the pack was played, he offered to take on all bettors against Keith.

One man eyed him incredulously. "You are giving odds against Omsbury? Lord, but you're daft . . . and here is my marker for a thousand pounds . . . Omsbury to win!"

Ben smiled and began recording the bets. It was about this time that Jewelene still disguised as Babette meandered to his side to watch the game. A worried glance was sent Keith's way, but he caught it and sent it to the winds. And then his eyes flickered. He heard in the background a familiar voice and scanned the room to find two newcomers had arrived. With a set purpose he gave them his back as he adjusted his seat.

"Eh?" said one of the newcomers, a tall gaunt fellow of some eight and twenty years, "what's afoot there, Bill?"

"Looks to me like they have an écarté game in full swing," answered his friend.

"By Jove, who would have thought it . . . I mean . . . écarté . . . the pugilism match and all . . . damn glad you talked me into this. Come on, let's go get our bets in . . ." then as he moved towards the assembled group, he saw a familiar profile. "Eh . . . well . . . I'll be damned . . . Rob! Robby, you old dog!"

The Honorable Oscar Robendale turned his pudgy face and opened wide his bright eyes, "Hello! You here, Tony?"

Robby was taken by the shoulders and shaken in a friendly fashion, all beneath the whimsical expression of Jewelene.

" 'Course I'm here . . . and Bill too. Still got eyes in your head, don't you? What's toward . . . who . . . egad! Keith here too? Won't interrupt him during the game though . . . but how do you both happen to come to Wight? Pugilism match, no doubt?"

"Er, yes . . ." said Robby uneasily. He still had no idea Babette and Jewelene were one and the same. But he was very certain that this was no time to blast their real identities about.

"Who is that he is playing?" asked Tony.

" 'Tis Lord Omsbury," said Tony's friend. "Considered to be a top sawyer."

"Is he? But . . . there is none better than the marquess there, is there, Robby?"

"Er . . . no . . ."

Jewelene was frowning for she had heard every word. What meant this fellow calling Keith the marquess?

"Why, the Marquess of Lyndhurst is the best écarté player in all of London!" continued Tony merrily.

"Shh . . ." said Rob, ". . . might ruin the betting, you know . . ."

Babette fluttered her lashes at Tony. "Ah, m'sieur . . . this marquess, surely you are mistaken . . . you speak to the marquess, no?"

Tony looked at her and then at Rob, "Speak to the . . . good God, no this is Oscar Robendale. That . . ." he said, pointing towards Keith, *"is the marquess."*

"I see. My . . . mistake," said Babette, turning her back upon them and flouncing out of their sight.

"Now you've done it!" said Robby in some disgust. "Keith didn't want the chit to know."

"Oh?" Then as he believed he understood, "Ooohooo."

Keith heard none of this exchange as they were some distance away and he was deep in concentration over the game. In addition there was a great deal of buzzing, betting, and jesting around his head, enough to block out all else. However, he saw out of the corner of his eye, an inflamed black-haired beauty pick up her skirts and dash out of the room. He saw too a look of consternation come over Robby's face, and an expression of surprise over Tony's, and he frowned. But the game recalled his attention.

Jewelene was livid. She scarcely knew what she did as she picked up her cloak and dashed out of the Silver Heart. Her vision was blurred as she ran the distance to the stables. Here, she found the stableboy asleep and without rousing him she led her mare out of the stall, and saddled her. Tightening the girth took but a moment, and a severe scold to her horse who would play games. Then she was up in the saddle still masked and bewigged and taking the street at a reckless pace.

Her heart felt as though it would burst, but she was angry too. He had made fools of them all . . . for what purpose, she did not know and did not care. He had come to their home and deliberately lied, and . . . and . . . he had led her to believe . . . he cared. She hated him. He was hell's minion, he was, and as Jewelene raced her horse over the fields she thought her heart had indeed burst into irretrievable pieces.

Just before she reached the Henshaw estate, she whipped off the wig and mask. She scrambled off her horse and took off its saddle. She would let her roam free tonight, she could send a groom for her in the morning. Safer than taking her into the stable at such an hour, and then once again she was scrambling up her trellis to her open window. Once safely inside she scanned the room without seeing, and then suddenly her legs gave way, her spirit gave way, and she sank to the floor. Her sobs were muffled only by her arms.

At the Silver Heart the écarté game was drawing to a close. Omsbury had never gained more than two plays since the first set. Five voles and several tricks had gone to the marquess, and everyone was tensely waiting to see who would win the deciding trick.

The marquess turned over a queen, and a gasp went round the room for the kings had already been taken. There was naught Omsbury could do, the trick went to the marquess; he needed now but one more to make the fifth and gain the final vole. Another queen to the marquess and the sound of thunder went round, for many a man lost with Omsbury in that moment.

Ben Clay smiled to himself as he called for the betting book. His instincts had led him to take on the bets against the marquess, and he was well pleased with his own judgment as well as the marquess's skill. More than the debt he owed Omsbury had been riding on the outcome of such a heavy game.

Keith pushed back his chair, ignoring the compliments that came flooding his way even from the men who had lost that evening. His gaze was intent on Omsbury. He had set out to beat this man and was well pleased. "That makes it 10,000 pounds, my lord," said the marquess quietly.

"I am well aware of it," said Omsbury unflinchingly. "You will, of course, accept my marker until the end of this week?"

The marquess nodded and stretched as he got to his feet. He scanned the room leisurely, frowning when he did not find Jewelene. Robby had already reached his side by this time, bringing up Tony in the rear.

"Hello, Keith, old boy!" greeted Tony, giving the marquess a slap on the back. "You remember Bill here, don't you?"

Keith smiled amicably. "Of course, how are you, Bill? Both here for that match next week, no doubt?"

"Aye, that's it," said Robby, "but . . ."

"Robby, have you seen Babette?" interrupted Keith.

"That's what I was trying to tell you . . . look, Keith, you ain't going to like this . . . thing is, not sure I like it.

Mind now, didn't want to do the thing in the first place, but now that we have . . ."

"Robby! If you don't mean to have me irritated beyond endurance . . ." started Keith on a laugh.

"Getting to it. Just don't know how to tell you . . ."

"Tell me what?" demanded Keith, now somewhat exasperated.

"It was quite unintentional, old boy," put in Tony. "Never knew you were playing fast and loose . . ."

The marquess's eyes narrowed. "What are you trying to tell me?"

"Tony here blabbed!" sighed Robby wearily. "There, knew you wouldn't like it . . . Babette didn't seem to like it either . . ."

"Damnation!" was all his friends heard him say before he stalked out.

Twenty-two

The Marquess of Lyndhurst mounted his roan and took to the open road. His temper was growing steadily blacker. He felt the fates had used him harshly, or so he told his horse.

"Fiend seize Tony for his blabbing! If anything was ever so ill-timed! Hell and damnation! The devil is in it that she won't listen to reason. So . . . what to do? What to do?"

His worthy animal appeared dumb on the subject, so he searched his mind, but by the time he had put his horse in the Henshaw stables and made his way to the house, indoors and up the stairs to his bedroom, he had not found a viable answer to so important a query. He slung off his cravat and dropped off his coat. It was a problem, but one thing he knew for sure. He would not make any attempt to speak with her tonight. Lord, no, that would be a mistake. He would wait until morning when she was calmer, when her anger had abated. Then he would approach her.

He knew her—but not quite well enough. For this was precisely the thing to add fuel to Jewelene's burning wrath. It was almost like chucking kindling twigs into the fire. She was waiting in her room, waiting for him to storm her door, waiting for him to offer her a reasonable explanation for his unspeakable behavior. She waited, and he did not come.

A new morn brought a dreary sky to overshadow the lovely Isle of Wight. Jewelene had not slept well, and she padded over to the window with a weary sigh. A soft drizzle beat down the tall blades of overgrown grass, and a wind was swishing a path through them with unwonted vigor. Her dreams had been painful and, though anger held her tears in check, they were there, waiting to be shed.

A knock sounded at her door, and she looked its way. "Yes?" she said slowly.

" 'Tis me," said her brother on the other side.

"Well then, come in love," she said straightening up, pulling her silk wrap around her, and fastening it in place with its sash.

Sir James appeared, a sunny smile on his face, his eyes alight with anticipation of the new day. "Wanted to stop by . . . we're off, you know," he said hesitantly. This was it, then. He and Arthur were taking Lightning off to Derby. Everything rested on Lightning's winning the race.

Jewelene rose to her feet. "Today . . . *now?* I thought you were not leaving until tomorrow?"

"That's what we set about . . ." he started.

"Oh, my God! Then you suspect Omsbury will try something. Oh, no, Jimmy . . ." she interrupted him.

He patted her arm. "Not to worry. Little brother will handle this."

Again she interrupted him. "But Jimmy, what if . . ."

"*Certes,* girl, been trying to tell you why I *don't* think we'll have any trouble. Art and I set it about that we weren't leaving until tomorrow. In fact . . . did it when we knew Jenkins was about. So, our leaving now is a good thing. We'll have a day's start on the scoundrels should they have any notions in their heads—and what's more—we'll be armed!"

"Does Jonas go with you?" she asked hopefully.

"Aye," he said, leaving out the details. No sense to worry her with such things.

She hugged him fiercely for a moment and, though he was taken aback by it and a certain despondency in her, he said little else before he took his leave. She sat for a long while afterward, but her thoughts had reverted from Lightning to a far different being.

"All right then, Jenkins . . . you understand. I don't want him hurt!" said Lord Omsbury. "You are to do it just as I outlined for you . . . no innovations on your own."

"Aye. Wot makes me worthy, m'lord, is that I knows 'ow to do yer bidding, I does."

"And what of your ruffians? Will they do my bidding?" asked Omsbury, raising his brow.

"Aye. They be stout boys at heart. I best be making tracks, m'lord, if me and the lads are to be in waiting for Sir James this night."

"Yes. That was, by the way, a brilliant little thing you did," said Omsbury, dropping an extra coin into his groom's palm.

"I thunk somethin' was wrong when Sir James sees me and then, as loud as ye please, starts blabbering about taking his horse to Derby tomorrow. 'Twere an easy thing to check at the dock and see when he hired a boat for . . ."

"Yes. Now off with you and remember . . ." warned Omsbury, "his signet ring and the horse's martingale . . ."

"Aye, m'lord . . . it will be done . . ." said Jenkins, smiling.

Omsbury turned his back on the man and did not bother to watch him go. Instead he gazed out of his library window and looked at the sea and thought of Jewelene.

Softly he spoke, "Soon, my beauty . . . very soon we will be together!" but not in a lover's voice.

The Marquess of Lyndhurst was up early that morning. He had already gone in to see Robby, who declared himself too ashamed to rise from bed to face Mrs. Debbs. Therefore, it would be Keith's job to see the thing through . . . alone.

It was not an easy task. Mrs. Debbs was much shocked to find that two grown men had played such a prank upon an entire household—and for a reason she found not at all logical. However, the marquess had managed to regain her esteem by announcing his love and intentions toward her niece.

"Marry her?" ejaculated Mrs. Debbs, at once surprised and delighted.

"Yes, madam . . . if you have no objection?" he said quietly.

"Why . . . no . . . but Jewelene . . . what does she say to you?"

"I have yet to find out. I rather fear she will at first be angry with me . . . but fancy she will come round," he said confidently.

"Do you?" she said rather doubtfully.

"Don't *you*?" he asked, raising a dark brow.

She gazed at his ginger hair, at his handsome face and arrogant chin. He was certainly a fine figure of a man, and she had noticed more than once that her niece seemed attracted to him. But she knew Jewelene, and Jewelene would not like having been duped. "Well . . ." she began, but was spared the necessity of further comment as the doors flew open to admit her niece.

Jewelene stopped at the threshold of the parlor and

stared angrily at his lordship. She was not aware that he knew of her discovery regarding his identity; however, she was all too acutely aware that he had let her go last night, had not come in search of her, had not attempted her room, had not in any way tried since then to resume the very audacious (and she was sure most improper) line of conversation he had started last night. And here he was, evidently awake and closeted with her aunt. What was he up to? She made up her mind to expose him before her Aunt Dora.

"Good morning, Auntie," she said gaily enough, turning only halfway toward his lordship and saying derisively, "and *my lord* . . . up so early . . . after such a night?"

"Indeed, I have been waiting for you to make an appearance on the chance that you might allow me to accompany you on an early morning ride," he said smoothly, his eyes intently watching hers.

Jewelene's eyes flashed at him, and he was amused, though he made a excellent attempt to steady his quivering lip.

"Did you think there was a chance of that, *my lord?* How doltish to be sure!"

"Jewelene!" said her aunt in shocked accents.

Unabashed, Jewelene turned a sweet countenance toward Mrs. Debbs. "Oh, I daresay you are surprised at me . . . referring to the gentleman you previously knew to be Mr. Robendale as 'my lord.' But you know, Auntie, we have all been quite muddled here at Henshaw House. You see before you the Marquess of Lyndhurst!"

"I know, dear . . ." sighed her aunt.

"To be sure, it comes as a great shock . . . after all . . ." She stopped and stared at her aunt, *"You know?* How do you know?"

"His lordship has just been explaining."

"His lordship has just been explaining . . ." repeated her niece, somewhat taken aback. "Why, how very clever of him." She gave him a mock curtsy.

He moved towards her. "Jewelene . . . let me explain . . ."

"*No!* Don't try your gammon on me, my lord. You will not find me so very gullible this time," and she gave him her back. "Please excuse me, ma'am . . ." she darted across the room to the door and left it swinging behind her.

The Marquess of Lyndhurst heaved a sigh, and Aunt Dora offered, "You see, my lord . . . she will not be won over easily. She has her father's high spirits and sense of fair play."

"And obviously she feels *I* have been playing dirty?" he said ruefully.

"Precisely so," said Aunt Dora putting a finger to her pursed lips.

"This is not where we made that wrong turn last time, and well you know it!" snapped Sir James.

"Don't know anything of the sort! Wouldn't have wondered about it, if I did know . . . now, would I? Don't stand to reason," said Arthur.

Sir James stared at him but said only, "Well, come on then."

"Tell you what, Jimmy . . . hungry. Very hungry!" replied Arthur.

Jimmy thought this over and decided it was not an unreasonable request. He had himself swallowed very little breakfast, and it was now well past noon. "There is an inn, I believe, another mile or so up the road. We'll stop there . . ."

"What of Jonas?"

"Lord, I don't know . . . I'll think of something by the time we get there. Come on."

And so they continued the journey, Lightning secure within their possession and little to fear in daylight.

"Jewelene . . . wait!" there was something in his tone that made her spin around and glare at him. But she did wait.

He'd been trying to catch her alone most of the day. Finally, he saw her go out toward the west woods, and he would not allow her to escape him now. He caught her arm and pulled her towards him. "You little fool . . . making us both miserable . . ." and then his lips were on hers, taking her breath away.

She was too angry to hear her heart. She was too consumed with a sense of hurt to hear the meaning of his words. Sh did the only thing she could in her pain. She raised her hand and struck a stinging slap across his cheek. He was taken aback by the viciousness of it. He stood a moment staring down at her. He saw no tears, no hurt, only burning anger, and it inflamed his own volatile temper. "Little vixen!" he hissed, "won't you listen to me?"

"Listen? To what . . . more lies?" she hissed back.

He pulled himself up. Very well, he thought. If she was going to be a spitfire hellcat, so be it! "It seems, Miss Henshaw, I was mistaken in you." At that he turned on his heel and left her standing.

She watched him go, and her eyes seemed mesmerized by his retreating form, but a little voice inside taunted her, and one large tear traced a line down her white cheek.

* * *

"But Elizabeth . . . she will not object when she hears of my plan," said Ben, holding his beloved's hand.

"Ben, you do not know mother . . ."

"But I do, and she was right not wanting you to make a match of it with a gaming hell owner. But I am selling the Silver Heart and at an excellent profit. Don't you understand?"

"I understand that she will then say you have no means of realizing an income. And oh, Ben, she will be quite right."

"But, darling, I have explained to you. With the profit from the Silver Heart, I shall be able to retire the mortgage against my father's lands . . . and more, I shall invest in the funds. We shall do, see if we won't."

She touched his cheek, "Oh, dearest Ben . . . all this . . . for me?"

He kissed her fervently. "Only for you."

Aunt Dora entered the sitting room at this juncture and, gasping, put a hand to her heart, "My God! what is the meaning of this?"

Jenkins eyed the tall, gaunt man before him thoughtfully. "So, you say there jest be the two of 'em at the inn? Wonder where that groom of his be? Well, well, this will be a piece of cake, lads. They'll be coming on their way soon . . . so up wit ye. We've got to mind our posts."

They took to saddle and two of the three men accompanying Jenkins traversed the narrow lone road on its other side. This section of the road curved through dense thickets. They had chosen their place well, and they had not long to wait.

They were forewarned by the frenzy of youthful conversation. Sir James and Arthur were arguing a set of points as loudly and as thoroughly as their youthful exuberance allowed. After all, they had nothing to fear, they knew the road's direction, 'twas broad daylight, and this time they were fairly certain they had not been followed.

And then all at once it happened. Riders came charging out of the bush surrounding them, waving pistols. Sir James bent toward his concealed weapon, but a heavy-set individual with an unruly shock of black hair displayed a amazing lack of teeth in his smile. "Aw now, guv', ye wouldn't 'ave in mind to fratch wit us?"

Sir James sneered at him but said nothing as he gazed round, attempting to buy time, attempting to see who it was did this thing by the light of day.

He only knew one thing, he would not give up Lightning. He would die first. If this was Omsbury's doing . . . he'd see to it that the villain would pay. Such thoughts kept his mind belligerent but not unaware, and there was something about the masked little man holding his horse in check some distance from the little band of cutthroats. And then he recognized Jenkins' voice, "Get his ring . . ."

"All right, guv', ye heard the man . . . heave over . . ." said the toothless fellow to Sir James.

"What? My ring?" said Sir James in some surprise thinking, what then? Not Lightning? Perhaps it wasn't Jenkins, perhaps it wasn't Omsbury's doing. He slid off his signet ring and dropped it into the man's dirty hand.

". . . the horse's martingale—and be quick!" hissed Jenkins impatient to be off.

Perturbed, Sir James watched them. Then he and Arthur were ordered off their horses, and they were secured to one another before the highwaymen were gone. As they worked the loosely bound ropes, Sir James frowned, "Odd that!"

"I'll say. Have a fat purse with me, Jimmy. They didn't even have a look-see!"

Twenty-three

It was some twenty minutes later that Sir James and Arthur had found themselves thoroughly entangled in the loosely tied rope. Each had done exactly the opposite to what they ought to have done, thus tightening the knots rather than loosening them.

"Fiend seize your stupidity!" thundered Sir James. "You've caused the blasted rope to cut into m'flesh! Dolt! Noddy! Stop pulling and groaning and sit still! Still, I say, or when I get out of this, I shall wring your skinny neck!"

Jonas, astride a very excellent gelding of some years, but well able to stand the strain of a long journey, came into view at this particular moment. He was studying the ground, noting the tracks, his dark eyes wary. If he was not mistaken, there had been some mighty strange doings in the last hour or so.

"Sh-h! Sh-h-h, I say!" shouted Jimmy suddenly at his friend who was at that moment giving him an account of the facts as he saw them. "Jonas . . . Jonas . . . that you?"

"Ayé, lad, where be ye?"

"In here . . . in here . . ." Jimmy and Art shouted in unison.

The older man was off his horse and rushing the thicket in a trice. "Upon my soul! Sir James! Did they hurt ye, lad . . . but here is Lightning!" said Jonas totally taken aback by such an unexpected piece of good fortune. He stroked the stallion's head. "Thar, thar, lovely, nobbut gonna hurt m'darlin boy. . . ."

"Jonas!" thundered Sir James, "undo these knots!"

"Oh . . . oh, aye, sir."

After some moments they were heartily congratulating Jonas for not dallying at the inn. "Then you didn't understand that silly stick Jimmy insisted on leaving as a message?" said Arthur unwisely.

Sir James glared at him, but as Jonas put in hastily, "Oh that! Saw the thing stuck in the ground, right in the middle of the road jest before I sighted the inn. Yes indeed . . . when I saw m'initial scratched into it, figured you wanted me to know you were stopping at the inn. Went inside m'self, but for no more than an ale and a cut of mutton. Didn't stay above ten minutes or so."

Sir James shot his friend a superior smile that did all he wished. Arthur was neatly buttoned for the moment. "Well, then, we had better get started. . . . ."

"But . . . it don't make sense do it, Sir James. I mean . . . it don't seem reet," uttered Jonas, scratching at his chin.

"What . . . you mean the fact that those scoundrels didn't take naught but m'signet ring and Lightning's martingale? No, it doesn't make any sense at all, but it don't signify. No doubt some fool prank or other. One thing is for sure . . . the marquess knew what he was about when he had you trail us rather than ride with us!"

"Aye," agreed Jonas, still deep in thought.

"One thing I still don't understand," put in Arthur. "Why was the marquess calling himself Robendale?"

Sir James, who did not fully understand the marquess's explanation which Keith had offered the day before, thought it best to send his friend a cowering glare and keep silent. "Mount your horse and don't dawdle, we've already lost precious time!"

"Then be ye wanting me to ride reet wit ye, Sir James . . . and not some paces aback?" asked Jonas.

"Certainly! We know we haven't been followed and, if there are to be any more highwaymen, we had better have numbers and arms ready!" Thus, the afternoon saw three riders and one magnificent stallion making their way to Derby.

Some four hours later, Jenkins was once again on the Isle of Wight, standing in Omsbury's library, delivering to him the objects he had obtained earlier that day.

"Well done, Jenkins! You are worth your hire, my man!" said Omsbury, well pleased. He moved to the bell-rope and gave it a tug. A moment later a lackey appeared and noted that his master seemed in excelent spirits. "You will go with this letter and . . ." he handed the boy the letter and a small plain box, "this package to Henshaw House. There you will give both to Miss Jewelene Henshaw and none other. You will see both delivered to her, or you will not leave. Understood?"

The young boy nodded and took the things his lordship handed him. "Right away, m'lord."

Lord Omsbury was smiling broadly, and Jenkins was taken somewhat by surprise when he saw that gentleman actually cast his head back and indulge in a bout of laughter.

It was late afternoon, and Jewelene had hidden herself away in her room. She was sulking. She was glad she had managed to insult the villain Lyndhurst! Perhaps now he would go. Yet such a thought made her utterly miserable. A knock sounded and she called admittance.

Her small maid appeared. "Sorry, miss, but this lad from Lord Omsbury has a package and a letter. Insists on delivering it to you personally. He be afraid to go back without having done the thing . . ."

Jewelene wanted nothing from Omsbury. But she was not so unfeeling as to allow his servants to suffer by her moods. "Oh, very well . . ."

The boy came in bowing and was instructed to leave the box and letter atop her vanity. He did so and bowed himself out. She smiled and called to her maid to give him a gratuity before he departed. Then, she surprised herself by her own curiosity. She got up and went to the letter, broke the seal and read:

My dearest Jewelene,

I had not wanted to win you by such means. However, for me the end must always justify the means. Have you I must, therefore, you will find in the container accompanying this letter, the reason you will meet me tonight.

Your brother's ring and your horse's martingale I give you as proof that I hold both within my power. Neither will be released until you are my wife in fact, not in promise. I take no chances, you see. I have ready the special license, and the minister willing to perform the ceremony.

Do not think I would not destroy what I cannot get! Mark me, Jewelene, if you want your brother free to enter his horse and attain financial independence, be at the crossroads tonight at eight. I shall be waiting with my coach. Bring nothing save yourself as it will be my pleasure to provide for you as your husband.

Yours,
Omsbury

Jewelene crumpled the letter in her hand and let it drop to the floor beside the hearth. Her hands trembled as she undid the box lid and found the black onyx ring that had been her father's and which now belonged to James. He was never without it . . . and then she picked up the brass martingale, a present from Ben. Oh God! Even for fighters who never say die . . . there is the moment when they know all is lost. For Jewelene this was that moment.

It was just about this time that Jonas made his mind to it and advised his master, "Thought it out . . . going back!"

"What?" ejaculated Sir James. "Why?"

"Must. Don't like it . . . them coves stealing your ring . . . not your diamond pin there, nor that large emerald ye be wearing, Mr. Arthur, but your papa's ring, lad . . . that spell somethin' I canna like! Omsbury be wishful of snapping up Miss Jewelene . . ."

"Yes, but he won't be able to do that without stopping Lightning from racing. . . ."

"What if she were to think he *did* stop Lightning from racing? What if he were to make her think . . . maybe ye was in danger . . .?"

Sir James stared at him hard a long moment before slapping his leg, "By Jove!"

"What's this?" asked Arthur, still trying to understand and somewhat astonished to see that Sir James seemed to comprehend already what the groom was talking about.

"Well then, hurry, man, hurry. Have you enough blunt?" said Sir James, ignoring his friend's query.

"Aye. Then I'm off . . . but, think on it . . . I'll

change m'horse at the posting house for a fresh filly, change it about on m'way back. Reet?"

"Right!" agreed Sir James, waving him off.

"What? Why . . . where is he going?" asked Arthur.

Dinner was a miserable meal. Only Robby seemed cheerful, but then only Robby had reason. He saw at once that Mrs. Debbs did not hold him in contempt, but rather treated him like some naughty boy discovered in a saucy but forgivable prank. Then too, Jewelene, whom he admired, seemed not to find fault with him, and best of all was that Lyla, who had discovered the truth, took to snubbing him, leaving him comfortably alone.

Elizabeth and her mother were at odds over Ben and did not speak. Lyla directed most of her attention to Keith, though her thoughts were on Omsbury whom she had seen on the road that very day and managed to flirt with some ten minutes before he moved on. Mrs. Debbs said very little and Jewelene nothing at all.

Keith watched her most intently, for there was something about her eyes; they seemed almost lifeless, and this was something new in Jewelene. Her hands moved nervously, and she was on edge. This was not because of their falling out. He just knew it could not be. But what then?

Elizabeth spoke quietly to Jewelene and, through her own troubles, saw that Jewelene was deeply disturbed over something. She tried drawing her out. "Jewelene . . . what is it?"

Jewelene's eyes fluttered in spite of herself to Keith's face. Stupid, she told herself. What can he do? Naught . . . naught, no one can do anything. Omsbury has Jimmy . . . and I must marry Omsbury. 'Tis ended. "Nothing," said she quietly. "I . . . think I'll go up and lie down," and then she was gone from the table.

Lyla chattered on, but Keith was not listening. He was watching Jewelene leave—watching and wondering what best to do.

Omsbury's coach waited at the crossroads just past the Henshaw estate. From this point they had several choices of direction as four roads veered off from the green center mound. He was early for it was still ten minutes to the hour, but he got out of his coach and paced a bit. He had required no answering letter from Jewelene. To do so would have shown weakness; no, his was the better way he told himself now, yet in spite of his confidence, he knew moments of doubt.

And then he saw her. She walked briskly, bouncing in that manner oddly her own. Even swathed in her voluminous, dark cloak, he knew her. He went forward and took her arm, but she yanked it from him, and her eyes glared. "Don't you dare touch me," she hissed in a voice full of hatred and suppressed rage. "You have forced my hand, sir, not my heart. Never think for an instant I have resigned myself to you!"

He was no fool. He did not press the issue now. He could be patient.

"After you, love," he said mockingly, bowing his head, indicating his coach. Her spirit was admirable, but not to touch her? She would learn all in good time, for he intended to touch her a great deal.

She swept past him and climbed the steps of the coach, sinking into a corner, and staring out its small sealed window. He sat opposite, watching her profile, believing he understood, and not understanding at all. It was too much a game to him and not one in the least to her. Therein lay the basic difference.

In the Henshaw house sat Robby, Elizabeth, the marquess and Lyla. Mrs. Debbs had gone up to speak with Jewelene and see if all was well, for her maid had knocked upon her door and had not received a response.

Elizabeth moved gracefully to and fro and then came to take a seat beside the marquess. "You, sir, I am persuaded, will agree with me that Jewelene was not herself tonight?"

"Indeed, I do agree, but I supposed it to have something . . ."

"To have something to do about you being the marquess and all, yes, yes, I thought that at first. But no, there was something . . ."

At that moment Mrs. Debbs burst in on them. "Elizabeth . . . she is not there."

Instantly she had the attention of the entire room. Elizabeth said nothing as she swept past her mother and made for the stairs.

"Elizabeth, where are you going? She is not there."

"I know, mother. But I was told that she received a letter from Lord Omsbury earlier . . . I should like to see if *it* is still there."

Keith was already standing. Omsbury? She had received a letter from Omsbury?

And then Elizabeth reappeared with the box, its contents, and the crumpled letter. Her face was flushed and her manner agitated.

"Mother . . . my lord . . . only look what the villain has done!"

Jewelene watched the passing fields and knew their direction. He was taking her to Newport. It was a big enough town; no doubt he meant to have the wedding performed quickly and without the usual fuss. Oh God, could nothing yet save her from him?

"Jewelene, can you not find some pleasure in this? Will you not look at me? 'Tis because I love you. . . ."

She whirled on him then. "Love? You fool! You know no such emotion. Love? You lust for me . . . you cannot call that love! Do you not see . . . I . . . I cannot abide you. Marriage to you is repugnant to me. Knowing that, you would yet force me to it . . . and you say you love me?"

His jawline hardened. "Call it what you will. In the end you will yield."

She turned away from him again and said very quietly, "I shall not yield, my lord. I shall perish, and then you will not want me, indeed, you will wonder why ever you thought you did!"

He frowned, wondering what she meant by such words. Was it a threat against her own life? His brow went up. He would have to watch her carefully, though he doubted she was of such mettle.

At the Henshaw house Elizabeth read the letter and received various comments.

"Oh, no, she has stolen Omsbury!" wailed Lyla.

Mrs. Debbs found a nearby chair and sank down with an audible gasp. Robby had jumped to his feet and was looking toward the marquess who had been standing all the while. "The fiend!" spat Rob. "Keith . . . shall we ride after them?"

"Elizabeth," said the marquess, his voice deadly quiet, "the crossroads, he says . . . where may they lead?"

"To Yarmouth, Carisbrooke, Newport, and Cowes," she answered.

"Very well. To Yarmouth he would not go. Far too close . . . too many who know them both could spot them and get word to the family, and I am fairly certain even with his ace in hand he wants no interference. We are left with Cowes and Newport, for Carisbrooke is too small to supply his needs. Which then?" he debated aloud.

"Newport!" answered Lyla, surprising them all. All heads turned in her direction. She was upset. She did not want Omsbury to marry Jewelene. She had formed a girlish infatuation for the man and meant to do everything she could to prevent their marriage. "I met Lord Omsbury on the road today, he was returning from Newport . . . not Cowes, I am certain of it."

The marquess's eyes narrowed as he weighed this. Yes, he believed the girl was telling the truth. And if Omsbury had arranged for a minister and was returning from such an errand when he met Lyla . . .

He made up his mind and stalked to the door. Flinging it open, he stepped back much surprised, and somewhat impatient, to find there a delay in the form of Sir James's groom. "Jonas!" he exploded. "What the devil!"

"Ay, m'lord, 'tis me."

"Yes, but why, and be quick, man!' ordered the marquess.

"Happen, it's a good thing, since I can see somethin' is amiss, and happen it have somethin' to do with Sir James's ring," said the groom succinctly.

"Sir James's ring?" ejaculated the marquess. "What about it?"

"They was attacked on the road today . . . the tobys wot done it took naught but the master's ring and Lightning's martingale."

"Then Sir James is safely on his way to Derby?" asked Elizabeth.

"Yes, Miss, that he is."

"Thank God!" said Mrs. Debbs.

"Rob, you stay here with the women and keep them calm about Jewelene. Omsbury shall not have her, depend upon it!" said the marquess, and anyone who knew him well would not have doubted his words. He turned to the groom, "Come along, Jonas. I shall need you to convince your mistress that James is safe."

Omsbury helped Jewelene alight from the carriage. A small white thatched-roof cottage stood before them. Its courtyard housed a neat compact stable; however, Omsbury made no use of it tonight. He did not plan to remain above twenty minutes. He led his bride to the doors, and a fluttering maid bade them welcome before vanishing in search of her mistress.

A few moments elapsed during which Omsbury paced about the small but delicately furnished chamber in some impatience. Jewelene, her dark cloak tightly clasped round herself, its hood still hanging low over her eyes, sat in quiet dejection. Soon, very soon all dreams, all hopes would be obliterated from her vision.

The door opened quietly. Jewelene did not look up though Omsbury spun round. He found there not the vicar he had met with earlier that day, but the vicar's wife. She was a small but robust woman. Her clipped gray curls were partially concealed by an ivory lace cap. Her cheeks were full and eyes bright. A pair of spectacles had slipped down low over her nose. Jewelene heard the rustle of the woman's muslin skirts and looked up curiously.

She had extended her hand to his lordship, her face a gentle, smiling apology. "I am so sorry, my lord. The vicar told me of his appointment with you. Please, have a seat. He should return shortly, and I have sent for refreshments which I hope you will enjoy until he can get himself away. We have a mare foaling, you see . . . but they did send me word that all goes well. He should be back shortly."

A tray was brought in at that moment, and the vicar's wife instructed the young serving girl to leave it. She lifted the teapot, scanning Jewelene's face, "Tea, my dear?"

"Oh, yes, thank you," said Jewelene, not wishing to be rude, though she was certain anything would taste bitter to her at this moment. The vicar's wife poured, chatting all the while, inviting his lordship to help himself to a glass of port if he so desired, noting with interest the manner in which Omsbury tossed it down.

All this while, some distance to the west rode a desperate man. The marquess felt a deadly white heat course through his veins. If Omsbury had succeeded, if the scoundrel had made Jewelene his wife . . . he had then bought himself a bullet. Dueling was illegal, killing your man would now mean banishment, especially if the man were as influential as Omsbury. However, the marquess made his plans knowing full well the consequences. No other would take Jewelene Henshaw to wife.

He thought of Jewelene. He loved her. With every beat of his heart he loved her. She had become his earth, his rain, his heaven and hell. Somehow almost mystically she had taken control. She had his very soul. Everything that made him what he was told him that she felt the same about him. And then they were entering Newport! But by God! It was bigger than he anticipated. Where . . . where had Omsbury gone?

"Oh," said the Mistress Shobert, listening intently, "I hear the vicar now." The door opened and a small, thin man with an abundance of white hair and bright eyes entered.

"A filly!" he said smacking his hands together. "So you owe me a crown, my dear!" he was bending, kissing his wife's cheek.

"Oh, you! I should know better than to wager against you. You have such luck!" said she smiling happily.

Omsbury nearly screamed in his impatience. "Do you think, Vicar Shobert, that we may get on with it?"

"What? Yes, yes, my lord . . ." He was now bending over Jewelene's hand. "So this is the lovely bride . . . so pleased, my dear . . ."

Omsbury nearly exploded with exasperation, "Vicar?"

"To be sure, to be sure . . . Ethel . . . get m'book . . . and m'spectacles. That's m'girl," he said smiling again at his wife.

Jonas was rubbing his chin. He had already taken his lordship to a bishop's establishment, and it proved fruitless, he was now racking his brains for he knew there was a vicar located somewhere about. Suddenly it came to him, "That's it. Remember it reet well. Come on then!" he said, leading the way.

It took them but a few minutes to go the short distance to Vicar Shobert's cottage, less to discover Omsbury's coach, and even less for the marquess' hand to land heavily on the front door.

"Dost thou, Jewelene . . . eh . . ." interrupting himself, the vicar turned toward his parlor door for he could hear a commotion going on in the hall. "What is happening, I wonder?"

"It doesn't matter. Get on with it!" snapped Omsbury.

"Dost thou, Jewelene Henshaw, take . . ." this time the words stopped as he dropped his jaw and turned again to his parlor door which had been flung open to admit a raging, ginger-haired man of considerable height and admirable lines.

"No, she does not!" thundered the marquess, crossing to take up Jewelene's arm and draw her to his side, shielding her with his own body.

He was here! It was like a miracle—he was really here, saving her from the fate she would have . . . but it was useless! He didn't understand, she must marry Omsbury. "No, let me go, Keith . . . you don't know what you are doing. I must marry Omsbury . . ."

Omsbury smiled dangerously. "You have heard her, are you now satisfied that I have not abducted Miss Henshaw?"

"I don't think I can be satisfied until I've let your blood!" and the marquess let go with his right. It caught Omsbury in the midsection, and then an upper cut from Keith's left sent the baron reeling backward into the furniture.

The vicar's wife screamed, and the vicar slammed down his prayerbook.

"Now just a moment here! I shall not allow such things to occur beneath my roof and in my wife's presence."

The marquess made him an apologetic bow. "I regret,

sir, taking such action beneath your roof . . . and in your lady's company. But this gentleman, and I use the word loosely, has seen fit to force this young woman into a situation she finds . . . unwelcome. Now if you don't mind, I should like to make very certain it does not happen again. You may continue with the ceremony, with but one change . . . the bridegroom!" He took out his card and handed it to the dumbfounded vicar.

"Stop it!" cried Jewelene. "You are spoiling everything, Keith. 'Tis not so simple . . ."

"Jonas, tell her how very simple!" smiled the marquess.

Jonas told his story quickly and when he was done Jewelene turned to Omsbury, and said quietly but firmly, "Good by, my lord!"

He sneered. It had become a useful device. It saved him face now, or so he believed. He made a mocking bow and left them. Jewelene turned to Keith. "How can I thank you?"

"Marry me."

She ran to his arms and he held her. Jonas coughed. The vicar turned to his wife who sighed. "Vicar, I am most pleased, are you not also? For I must admit having formed a considerable degree of dislike for that other gentleman. And is *this* not more romantic?"

He patted her hand, but turned to the two young people who had evidently forgotten their presence. "Ahem!"

Jewelene and the marquess parted, blushing, and he frowned at them, " 'Twould appear to me that you two are ready! What's more, the wedding has been paid for . . . the special license in hand . . . well, 'twould seem to me . . ."

". . . that a wedding is in order," said the willing groom drawing his bride's arm through his. "Proceed, good sir!"

*   *   *

And what of later? There is always the business of what then came. Lightning did, in fact, win his race. Sir James went with Arthur Salford in the fall to Cambridge, leaving Jonas to breed the stallion at home. Elizabeth was married to Ben Clay, and her mother became resigned to it if not jubilant. And of Jewelene and her ginger-haired marquess? 'Twould be romantic fiction to tell they 'lived happily ever after,' but indeed, they came close to it— very close.

ALL AT $1.75!

Enduring romances that represent a rich reading experience.

BABE by Joan Smith	50023
THE ELSINGHAM PORTRAIT by Elizabeth Chater	50018
FRANKLIN'S FOLLY by Georgina Grey	50026
THE HIGHLAND BROOCH by Rebecca Danton	50022
A LADY OF FORTUNE by Blanche Chenier	50028
LADY HATHAWAY'S HOUSE PARTY by Jennie Gallant	50020
THE LORD AND THE GYPSY by Patricia Veryan	50024
THE LYDEARD BEAUTY by Audrey Blanshard	50016
THE MATCHMAKERS by Rebecca Baldwin	50017
A MISTRESS TO THE REGENT by Helen Tucker	50027
REGENCY GOLD by Marion Chesney	50002
WAGER FOR LOVE by Rachelle Edwards	50012

Buy them at your local bookstore or use this handy coupon for ordering.

COLUMBIA BOOK SERVICE (a CBS Publications Co.)
32275 Mally Road, P.O. Box FB, Madison Heights, MI 48071

Please send me the books I have checked above. Orders for less than 5 books must include 75¢ for the first book and 25¢ for each additional book to cover postage and handling. Orders for 5 books or more postage is FREE. Send check or money order only.

Cost $_____   Name _____

Postage_____   Address _____

Sales tax*_____ City _____

Total $_____   State _____ Zip _____

*The government requires us to collect sales tax in all states except AK, DE, MT, NH and OR.

This offer expires 1/31/81   8000-4